This book belongs to

- -

ACC CHILDREN'S CLASSICS

an imprint of
Antique Collectors' Club Ltd
5 Church Street, Woodbridge,
Suffolk 1P12 1DS, UK
and
Market Street Industrial Park, Wappingers' Falls,
NY 12590, USA

Sailing Days first published 1998
Compiled by Amy McKay

ISBN 1 85149 703 X

British Library Cataloguing-in-Publication Data
A catalogue record for this book is available from the British Library

Published and printed in England
on Consort Royal Satin paper
from Donside Mills, Aberdeen
by Antique Collectors' Club Ltd.

SAILING DAYS

Stories and Poems
about Sailors and the Sea

Compiled by Amy McKay

ACC CHILDREN'S CLASSICS

CONTENTS

Section One

MESSING ABOUT IN BOATS

CASTING OFF
AND
SETTING SAIL

from

THE WIND IN THE WILLOWS
by Kenneth Grahame

PART I

Never in his life had he seen a river before — this sleek, sinuous, full-bodied animal, chasing and chuckling, gripping things with a gurgle and leaving them with a laugh, to fling itself on fresh playmates that shook themselves free, and were caught and held again. All was a-shake and a-shiver — glints and gleams and sparkles, rustle and swirl, chatter and bubble. The Mole was bewitched, entranced, fascinated. By the side of the river he trotted as one trots, when very small, by the side of a man, who holds one spellbound by exciting stories; and when tired at last, he sat on the bank, while the river still chattered on to him, a babbling procession of the best stories in the world, sent from the heart of the earth to be told at last to the insatiable sea.

As he sat on the grass and looked across the river, a dark hole in the bank opposite, just above the water's edge, caught his eye, and dreamily he fell to considering what a nice snug dwelling-place it would make for an animal with a few wants and fond of a bijou riverside residence, above flood-level and remote from noise and dust. As he gazed, something bright and small seemed to twinkle down in the heart of it, vanished, then twinkled once more like a tiny star. But it could hardly be a star in such an unlikely situation; and it was too glittering and small for a glow-worm. Then, as he looked, it winked at him, and so declared itself to be an eye; and a small face began gradually to grow up round it, like a frame round a picture.

A brown little face, with whiskers.

A grave round face, with the same twinkle in its eye that had first attracted his notice.

Small neat ears and thick silky hair.

It was the Water Rat!

Then the two animals stood and regarded each other cautiously.

'Hullo, Mole!' said the Water Rat.

'Hullo, Rat!' said the Mole.

'Would you like to come over?' enquired the Rat presently.

'Oh, it's all very well to *talk*,' said the Mole, rather pettishly, he being new to a river and riverside life and its ways.

The Rat said nothing, but stooped and unfastened a rope and hauled on it; then lightly stepped into a little boat which the Mole had not observed. It was painted blue outside and white within, and was just the size for two animals; and the Mole's whole heart went out to it at once, even though he did not yet fully understand its uses.

The Rat sculled smartly across and made fast. Then he held up his forepaw as the Mole stepped gingerly down. 'Lean on that!' he said. 'Now then, step lively!' and the Mole to his surprise and rapture found himself actually seated in the stern of a real boat.

'This has been a wonderful day!' said he, as the Rat shoved off and took to the sculls again. 'Do you know, I've never been in a boat before in all my life.'

'What?' cried the Rat, open-mouthed. 'Never been in a — you never— well, I— what have you been doing, then?'

'Is it so nice as all that?' asked the Mole shyly, though he was quite prepared to believe it as he leant back in his seat and surveyed the cushions, the oars, the rowlocks, and all the fascinating fittings, and felt the boat sway lightly under him.

'Nice? It's the *only* thing,' said the Water Rat solemnly, as he leant forward for his stroke. 'Believe me, my young friend, there is *nothing* — absolutely nothing — half so much worth doing as simply messing about in boats. Simply messing,' he went on dreamily: 'messing — about — in boats; messing —'

'Look ahead, Rat!' cried the Mole suddenly.

It was too late. The boat struck the bank full tilt. The dreamer, the joyous oarsman, lay on his back at the bottom of the boat, his heels in the air.

'— about in boats — or *with* boats,' the Rat went on composedly, picking himself up with a pleasant laugh. 'In or out of 'em, it doesn't matter. Nothing seems really to matter, that's the charm of it. Whether you get away, or whether you don't; whether you arrive at your destination or whether you reach somewhere else, or whether you never get anywhere at all, you're always busy, and you never do anything in particular; and when you've done it there's always something else to do, you can do it if you like, but you'd much better not. Look here! If you've really nothing else on hand this morning, supposing we drop down the river together, and have a long day of it?'

The Mole waggled his toes from sheer happiness, spread his chest with a sigh of full contentment, and leaned back blissfully into the soft cushions. '*What* a day I'm having!' he said. 'Let us start at once!'

Boating

by James Reeves

Gently the river bore us
Beneath the morning sky,
Singing, singing, singing
Its reedy, quiet tune
As we went floating by;
And all the afternoon
In our small boat we lay
Rocking, rocking, rocking
Under the willows grey.

When into bed that evening
I climbed it seemed a boat
Was softly rocking, rocking
Rocking me to sleep,
And I was still afloat.
I heard the grey leaves weep
And whisper round my bed,
The river singing, singing,
Singing through my head.

from

THE LITTLE GREY MEN

by 'B.B.'

It took the gnomes some time to collect enough suitable wood, and longer still to portage it down the bank to the oak tree root. But at last the job was done and they began hammering, shaping and planing for all they were worth. They tapped like woodpeckers and worked so hard that when Dodder returned, still grumpily stumping along with his hands behind his back, and eyes on the ground, the boat was taking shape.

When he saw what they were doing he said nothing but went straight into the cave and did not come out again. The gnomes worked on until it was too dark to see. All the next day and the next they toiled, stopping only for a bite of food. By the end of the month the boat was nearly finished and looked something like this:

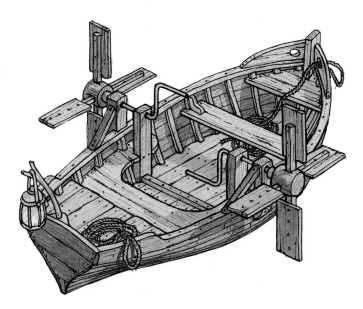

For paddles they used strips of wood, cleverly wedged into wooden hubs, and the two handles were made out of bent wire, filched from a fence. The bending of the wire was the most difficult job of all, for it took their united strength to hammer it to the right shape, the corner of the brook rang like a blacksmith's shop.

All the animals and birds up and down the stream had got wind of what was happening, for the tidings had been passed from beak to beak and from mouth to mouth. Everybody came to look at the new boat, for it was the finest boat ever built by gnomes.

As it neared completion it was tied up under a log which lay among the stinging nettles of the bank so that all could admire it. Baldmoney and Sneezewort were very proud of their handiwork for, as you can see, it was a splendid boat and very ingeniously made.

Even Dodder was secretly impressed. He used to go and peep at it when he thought the others were not looking. But still he refused to talk and went about with his eyes on the ground. Poor little gnome; secretly he wished that he was going too, for in all his life he had never been alone and the idea of the long summer months without his companions would not bear dwelling on. But he was of a very proud nature, and once gnomes make up their minds about a thing it takes a lot to change them.

By the first week in May the boat was finished. It was varnished with gum from a near-by sycamore and looked very smart and streamworthy. The launching was a great moment. Gnomes never waste time over anything. The boat was finished on the Second of May, at five o'clock in the evening, and at seven o'clock they decided to launch her in the pool. They put wooden rollers under her and tied a twisted grass rope to the prow. They pulled for all they were worth to get her down the bank, but they could not stir her. Baldmoney's feet kept slipping on the loose shingle. This held up matters for a bit, for of course Dodder was nowhere to be seen: he was sulking in the house. I doubt if they ever would have got her down the bank had not a passing toad lent a hand. They tied the grass halter round his neck and all three pulled and pulled. 'It's moving.' said Baldmoney excitedly; 'pull, you fellows, pull.' And sure enough the heavy little boat began to jerk forwards towards the stream, nearer and nearer to the water's edge until at last, with one final heave, it slid in with a faint splash. The trouble they had in getting the grass halter off the toad you wouldn't believe, for he kept trying to swim away. After a tremendous amount of splashing and noise they at last pulled the boat back to land and tied it up to a hawthorn bough. Then, thanking the toad, they went off to plead with Dodder.

They found him inside the house, right up in the corner by the cellar, and Baldmoney noticed that he had been crying. His eyes were very red, but he pretended it was the smoke from the fire.

'Come on Dodder, we're gong to try the boat. Toad helped us to launch her and she floats beautifully. We're going to paddle her up the Folly as far as the Stickle. *Do* come, Dodder!'

They coaxed and wheedled but the little man said no word and shook them off roughly. So they left him alone and went to try the boat.

It was late now, and Zene was out, flickering round over the water. The two gnomes were wildly excited as they climbed aboard. Sneezewort pushed off with a willow stick and the little boat swung gently into the current of the deep pool.

Looking upstream they saw the smooth water winding away towards the rapids, the reflections of the bushes and willows, dark and mysterious, at the bend in the brook.

A song thrush, singing among the white blackthorn blossom, stopped his song when he saw the boat pull out from the bank and sat watching the gnomes with interested eye.

Two male blackbirds who were running round each other in a love duel (their tails fanned and crests depressed) also saw the boat push off, and even they forgot their jealous anger and flew up to the oak tree to see how the gnomes fared.

Baldmoney took one of the paddle handles and Sneezewort the other and they began to turn them round. At first the gentle current still pushed the boat backwards but, as the paddles got to work, the backward movement ceased, the boat became stationary and then oh, joy! it began to slowly forge upstream.

As the gnomes got in their stride, each working his handle in rhythm, the boat gathered speed until it was steadily pushing a furl of water before it and heading up the centre of the pool.

Neither of the gnomes spoke. As they were bent over the handles they did not see the dim face of Dodder peering round one corner of the oak root. The poor little man could not resist coming to see how the boat worked. When Baldmoney stopped paddling for a moment to wipe away a bead of sweat from his brow Dodder immediately bobbed back into the shadow, for he didn't want to be seen.

Out of the corner of his eye Sneezewort saw the sturdy green rushes and young nettles growing on the opposite bank slowly sliding past. He worked with all his might, delighted with the success of the boat and with the ease with which it slid through the water. It was infinitely better than paddling one of the coracles.

But the test was yet to come. As they neared the Stickle the sound of the water furling against the prow of the boat loudened into a chuckle and a thin film swept over the bottom boards, wetting the gnomes' feet. But they worked with a will and inch by inch they crept upstream until the smooth water round the bend was reached.

They headed into the bank and tied up to an iris flag. 'Phew,' gasped Sneezewort, 'that was hard work. We can do it, but we shall have to get Watervole to help us at the rapids; unless we meet any bigger ones below Crow Wood we ought to get up without a lot of trouble.'

Baldmoney was sitting in the prow, mopping his forehead. 'Don't tell me I can't design boats, Sneezewort; we can go anywhere in this!'

adapted from

MOBY DICK

by Herman Melville

Now, when I say that I am in the habit of going to sea whenever I begin to grow hazy about the eyes, and begin to be over conscious of my lungs, I do not mean to have it inferred that I ever go to sea as a passenger. For to go as a passenger you must needs have a purse, and a purse is but a rag unless you have something in it. Besides, passengers get sea-sick — grow quarrelsome — don't sleep of nights — do not enjoy themselves much, as a general thing — no, I never go as a passenger; nor, though I am something of a salt, do I ever go to sea as a Commodore, or a Captain, or a Cook. I abandon the glory and distinction of such offices to those who like them. For my part, I abominate all honourable respectable toils, trials, and tribulations of every kind whatsoever. It is quite as much as I can do to take care of myself, without taking care of ships, barques, brigs, schooners, and what not. And as for going as cook, — though I confess there is considerable glory in that, a cook being a sort of officer on ship-board — yet, somehow, I never fancied broiling fowls — though once broiled, judiciously buttered, and judgmatically salted and peppered, there is no one who will speak more respectfully, not to say reverentially, of a broiled fowl than I will.

No, when I go to sea, I go as a simple sailor, right before the mast, plumb down into the forecastle, aloft there to the royal mast-head. True, they rather order me about some, and make me jump from spar to spar, like a grasshopper in a May meadow. And at first, this sort of thing is unpleasant enough. It touches one's sense of honour, particularly if you come of an old established family in the land. And more than all, if just previous to putting your hand into the tar-pot, you have been lording it as a country schoolmaster, making the tallest boys stand in awe of you. The transition is a keen one, I assure you, from a schoolmaster to a sailor. But even this wears off in time.

What of it, if some old hunks of a sea-captain orders me to get a broom and sweep down the decks? What does that indignity amount to, weighed, I mean, in the scales of the New Testament? Do you think the archangel Gabriel thinks any the less of me, because I promptly and respectfully obey that old hunks in that particular instance? Who aint a slave? Tell me that. Well, then, however the old sea-captains may order me about — however they may thump and punch me about, I have the satisfaction of knowing that it is all right; that everybody else in one way or other served in much the same way — either in a physical or metaphysical point of view, that is, and so the universal thump is passed round, and all hands should rub each other's shoulder blades, and be content.

Again, I always go to sea as a sailor, because they make a point of paying me for my trouble, whereas they never pay passengers a single penny that I ever heard of. On the contrary, passengers themselves must pay. And there is all the difference in the world between paying and being paid. The act of paying is perhaps the most uncomfortable infliction that the two orchard thieves entailed upon us. But *being paid*, — what will compare with it?

Finally, I always go to sea as a sailor, because of the wholesome exercise and pure air of the forecastle deck. For as in this world, head winds are far more prevalent than winds from astern, so for the most part the Commodore on the quarter-deck gets his atmosphere at second hand from the sailors on the forecastle. He thinks he breathes it first; but not so. But wherefore it was that after having repeatedly smelt the sea as a merchant sailor, I should now take it into my head to go on a whaling voyage; this is the invisible police officer of the Fates, who has the constant surveillance of me, and secretly dogs me, and influences me in some unaccountable way — he can better answer than any one else. And, doubtless, my going on this whaling voyage, formed part of the grand programme of Providence that was drawn up a long time ago.

THE VOYAGES OF DOCTOR DOLITTLE
by Hugh Lofting

That same week we began our preparations for the voyage. 'Suppose we go down and see your friend Joe, the mussel-man,' said the Doctor. 'He will know about boats.'

'I'd like to come too,' said Jip.

'All right, come along,' said the Doctor and off we went.

Joe said he had a boat — one he had just bought — but it needed three people to sail her. We told him we wanted to see it anyway.

So the mussel-man took us off a little way down the river and showed us the neatest, prettiest little vessel that ever was built. She was called the *Curlew*. Joe said he would sell her to us cheap. But the trouble was that the boat needed three people, while we were only two.

'Of course I shall be taking Chee-Chee,' said the Doctor. 'But although he is very quick and clever, he is not as strong as a man. We really ought to have another person to sail a boat as big as that.'

'There's Matthew Mugg, the cat's-meat man,' I said.

'No, he wouldn't do. Matthew's a very wise fellow, but he talks too much – mostly about his rheumatism. You have to be frightfully particular whom you take with you on long voyages.'

Well, in the end, the Doctor bought the *Curlew* and we began at once to provision her. And for three whole days we carried sacks of flour, kegs of treacle, tins of tea and every possible thing we could store in her hold.

Two days after that we had all in readiness for our departure.

On this voyage Jip begged so hard to be taken that the Doctor finally gave in and said he could come. Polynesia and Chee-Chee were the only other animals to go with us. Dab-Dab was left in charge of the house and the animal family we were to leave behind.

At the river wall we found a great crowd waiting to see us off.

Standing right near the gang-plank were my mother and father. I hoped that they would not make a scene, or burst into tears or anything

like that. But as a matter of fact they behaved quite well — for parents. My mother said something about being sure not to get my feet wet; and my father just smiled a crooked sort of smile, patted me on the back and wished me luck. Goodbyes are awfully uncomfortable things and I was glad when it was over and we passed on to the ship.

At last, after much pulling and tugging, we got the anchor up and undid a lot of mooring ropes. Then the *Curlew* began to move gently down the river with the out-running tide, while the people on the wall cheered and waved their handkerchiefs.

For me indeed it was a great and wonderful feeling, that getting out into the open sea, when at length we passed the little lighthouse at the mouth of the river and found ourselves free of the land. It was all so new and different; just the sky above you and the sea below. This ship, which was to be our house and our street, our home and our garden, for so many days to come, seemed so tiny in all this wide water — so tiny and yet so snug, sufficient, safe.

I looked around me and took in a deep breath. The Doctor was at the wheel steering the boat which was now leaping and plunging gently through the waves. (I had expected to feel seasick at first but was delighted to find that I didn't.) Chee-Chee was coiling up ropes in the stern and laying them in neat piles. My work was fastening down the things on the deck so that nothing could roll about if the weather should grow rough when we got farther from the land. Jip was up in the peak of the boat with ears cocked and nose stuck out — like a statue, so still — his keen old eyes keeping a sharp look-out for floating wrecks, sand-bars and other dangers. Each one of us had some special job to do, part of the proper running of a ship. Even old Polynesia was taking the sea's temperature with the Doctor's bath-thermometer tied on the end of a string, to make sure there were no icebergs near us. As I listened to her swearing softly to herself because she couldn't read the pesky figures in the fading light, I realised that the voyage had begun in earnest and that very soon it would be night — my first night at sea!

from

MOOMINPAPPA AT SEA

by Tove Jansson

translated by Kingsley Hart

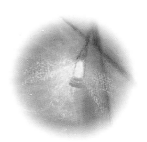

On the all-important evening of their departure, the wind had moved towards the east; it had got up soon after twelve, but they had decided not to leave before sunset. The sea was warm and deep blue, just as blue as it was in the crystal ball. The jetty was piled high with luggage, right up to the bathing-house, where the boat was lying tied-up. It was bobbing up, and down, with its sail hoisted and a hurricane lamp was burning at the top of the mast. On the beach it was already getting dark.

* * *

'Of course we run the risk of it being calm tonight,' said Moominpappa. 'We could have left immediately after lunch. But on an occasion like this we must wait for sunset. Setting out in the right way is just as important as the opening lines in a book: they determine everything.' He sat in the sand next to Moominmamma. 'Look at the boat,' he said. 'Look at the *Adventure*. A boat by night is a wonderful sight. This is the way to start a new life, with a hurricane lamp shining at the top of the mast, and the coast-line disappearing behind one as the whole world lies sleeping. Making a journey by night is more wonderful than anything in the world.'

'Yes, you're right,' replied Moominmamma. 'One makes a trip by day, but by night one sets out on a journey.' She was rather tired after all the packing, and a little worried in case something important had been forgotten. The pile of luggage looked enormous now that it was all there on the jetty, but she knew how little it would seem when they unpacked. A whole family needs such an awful lot of things in order to live through a single day in the proper way.

But now, of course, things were different. Now the proper thing to do was that they should begin an entirely new life, and that Moominpappa should provide everything they needed, look after them, and protect them. Life must have been too easy for them up till now. 'It's strange,' Moominmamma thought. 'Strange that people can be sad, and even angry because life is too easy. But that's the way it is, I suppose. The only thing to do is to start life afresh.'

'Don't you think it's dark enough now?' she said. 'Your hurricane lamp looks really lovely against the sky. Perhaps we might start now.'

'Just a moment, I must get my bearings,' said Moominpappa. He spread out the map on the sand and stared at the island, all by itself right out in the open sea. He was very serious. He sniffed in the wind for a while and tried to get his sense of direction, something he hadn't had to use for a long time. Our ancestors never needed to worry about finding the right course, it came to them naturally of its own accord. It's a pity that the instinct gets weaker if you don't use it.

After a while, Moominpappa felt that he was sure he had the right course. He knew which way to go, so they could set sail. He put his hat straight and said: 'Let's be off. But you're not to lift a thing. We'll do all the heavy work. Just go aboard.'

Moominmamma nodded, and somewhat wearily dragged herself to her feet. The sea had turned violet and the line of the forest along the shore looked soft and dark. She was very sleepy, and suddenly felt everything was a little unreal; a slow, fantastically lit dream in which one walks through heavy, heavy sand without getting anywhere.

The others were on the jetty, putting the luggage on board. The storm lantern swayed to and fro, and the silhouette of the jetty and the bathing-house looked like a long spiky dragon against the evening sky. She could hear Little My laughing, and behind her the cries of night birds still awake in the forest.

'It's so beautiful!' said Moominmamma to herself. 'Beautiful and just a little strange. Now I've time to think about it, the whole thing *is* rather wonderful. But I wonder whether Pappa will mind if I take a little nap in the boat.'

* * *

The Groke slunk through the garden after sunset, but this evening there was no lamp on the veranda. The curtains had been taken down and the water-butt had been turned upside down. The key hung on its nail above the door.

She was used to deserted houses, and she saw at once that no one would light a lamp here for a long time to come. She shuffled slowly back up the slope towards the cliff. For a moment the crystal ball caught her reflection, but then once more was filled with its usual, unreal deep blue. The forest caught its breath in fear as she approached, strange little sounds could be heard from under the moss, branches rustled with fright and the lights of tiny eyes went out everywhere. Without pausing, she went up to the top of the cliff overlooking the southern shore and gazed out over the sea, now growing dark as night fell.

She could see the hurricane lamp at the top of the mast of the *Adventure* quite clearly, a lonely star gliding past the last islands, all the time moving farther out towards the open sea.

She gazed at it for a long time for she was never in a hurry. Time for her was endless and passed very slowly. Time for her contained nothing, except the occasional lamps which were lit as autumn approached.

Now she glided down the ravine towards the beach. Behind her she left big shapeless footprints, as though a seal had dragged itself to the edge of the water. The waves drew back as she approached, and then hesitated as if they didn't know what to do next. The water became smooth and still round the dark hem of her skirt and began to freeze.

For a long time she stood there, while a cloud of freezing mist gathered round her. Now and then she slowly lifted one of her feet, and the ice crackled and became thicker and thicker. She was building an island of ice for herself in order to reach the hurricane lamp. It was out of sight behind the islands now, but she knew it was there somewhere. If it went out before she got to it, it wouldn't matter. She could wait. They would light another lamp some other evening. They always did sooner or later.

* * *

Moominpappa was steering the boat. He held the rudder tightly in one of his paws, feeling that he and the boat understood each other. He was completely at peace with himself. His family looked just as tiny and helpless as they had looked in the crystal ball; he was guiding them safely across the vast ocean through the silent, blue night. The hurricane lamp lit the way, just as if Moominpappa had drawn a firm bright line across the map, saying: 'from here... to there. That's where we're going to live. There my lighthouse will be the centre of the world, it will tower proudly above the dangers of the ocean at its feet.'

'You don't feel the cold, do you?' he shouted happily. 'Have you wrapped the blanket round you?' he asked Moominmamma. 'Look, we've left the last island behind us now, and soon it will be the darkest part of the night. Sailing at night is very difficult. You have to be on the look-out all the time.'

'Why of course, dear!' said Moominmamma, who was lying curled up in the bottom of the boat. 'This is all a great experience,' she thought. The blanket had got a little wet and she moved gingerly towards the windward side. But the ribs of the boat got in the way of her ears all the time.

Little My sat in the bow of the boat, humming monotonously to herself.

'Mamma,' whispered Moomintroll. 'What happened to her to make her like that?'

'Who?'

'The Groke. Did somebody do something to her to make her so awful?'

'No one knows,' said Moominmamma, drawing her tail out of the water. 'It was probably because nobody did anything at all. Nobody bothered about her, I mean. I don't suppose she remembers anyway, and I don't suppose she goes around thinking about it either. She's like the rain or the darkness, or a stone you have to walk round if you want to get past. Do you want some coffee? There's some in the thermos in the white basket.'

'Not just now,' said Moomintroll. 'She's got glassy eyes just like a fish. Can she talk?'

Moominmamma sighed and said 'No one talks to her, or about her either, otherwise she gets bigger and starts to chase one. And you mustn't feel sorry for her. You seem to imagine that she longs for everything that's alight, but all she really wants to do is to sit on it so that it'll go out and never burn again. And now I think I might go to sleep for a while.'

Pale autumn stars had come out all over the sky. Moomintroll lay on his back looking at the hurricane lamp, but he was thinking about the Groke. If she was someone you mustn't talk to or about, then she would gradually vanish and not even dare to believe in her own existence. He wondered whether a mirror might help. With lots and lots of mirrors one could be any number of people, seen from the front and from the back, and perhaps these people might even talk to each other. Perhaps...'

Everything was silent. The rudder creaked softly, and they all slept. Moominpappa was alone with his family. He was wide-awake, more wide-awake than he had ever been before.

from

THE WIND IN THE WILLOWS

PART II   by Kenneth Grahame

The afternoon sun was getting low as the Rat sculled gently homewards in a dreamy mood, murmuring poetry-things over to himself, and not paying much attention to Mole. But the Mole was very full of lunch, and self-satisfaction, and pride, and already quite at home in a boat (so he thought) and was getting a bit restless besides: and presently he said, 'Ratty! Please, *I* want to row, now!'

The Rat shook his head with a smile. 'Not yet, my young friend,' he said — 'wait till you've had a few lessons. It's not so easy as it looks.'

The Mole was quiet for a minute or two. But he began to feel more and more jealous of Rat, sculling so strongly and so easily along, and his pride began to whisper that he could do it every bit as well. He jumped up and seized the sculls, so suddenly, that the Rat, who was gazing out over the water and saying more poetry-things to himself, was taken by surprise and fell backwards off his seat with his legs in the air for the second time, while the triumphant Mole took his place and grabbed the sculls with entire confidence.

'Stop it, you *silly* ass!' cried the Rat, from the bottom of the boat. 'You can't do it! You'll have us over!'

The Mole flung his sculls back with a flourish, and made a great dig at the water. He missed the surface altogether, his legs flew up above his head, and he found himself lying on the top of the prostrate Rat. Greatly alarmed, he made a grab at the side of the boat, and the next moment — Sploosh!

Over went the boat, and he found himself struggling in the river.

Oh, my how cold the water was, and Oh, how *very* wet it felt. How it sang in his ears as he went down, down, down! How bright and welcome the sun looked as he rose to the surface coughing and spluttering! How black was his despair when he felt himself sinking again! Then a firm paw gripped him by the back of his neck. It was the Rat, and he was evidently laughing — the Mole could *feel* him laughing, right down his arm and through his paw and so into his — the Mole's — neck.

The Rat got hold of a scull and shoved it under the Mole's arm; then he did the same by the other side of him and, swimming behind, propelled the helpless animal to shore, hauled him out, and set him down on the bank, a squashy pulpy lump of misery.

When the Rat had rubbed him down a bit, and wrung some of the wet out of him, he said, 'Now then, old fellow! Trot up and down the towing-path as hard as you can, till you're warm and dry again, while I dive for the luncheon-basket.'

So the dismal Mole, wet without and ashamed within, trotted about till he was fairly dry, while the Rat plunged into the water again, recovered the boat, righted her and made her fast, fetched his floating property to shore by degrees, and finally dived successfully for the luncheon-basket and struggled to land with it.

When all was ready for a start once more, the Mole, limp and dejected, took his seat in the stern of the boat; and as they set off, he said in a low voice, broken with emotion, 'Ratty, my generous friend! I am very sorry indeed for my foolish and ungrateful conduct. My heart quite fails me when I think how I might have lost that beautiful luncheon-basket. Indeed, I have been a complete ass, and I know it. Will you overlook it this once and forgive me, and let things go on as before?'

'That's all right, bless you!' responded the Rat cheerily. 'What's a little wet to a Water Rat? I'm more in the water than out of it most days. Don't you think any more about it; and, look here! I really think you had better come and stop with me for a little time. It's very plain and rough, you know — not like Toad's house at all — but you haven't seen that yet; still, I can make you comfortable. And I'll teach you to row, and to swim, and you'll soon be as handy on the water as any of us.'

The Mole was so touched by his kind manner of speaking that he could find no voice to answer him; and he had to brush away a tear or two with the back of his paw. But the Rat kindly looked in another direction, and presently the Mole's spirits revived again, and he was even able to give some straight back-talk to a couple of moorhens who were sniggering to each other about his bedraggled appearance.

When they got home, the Rat made a bright fire in the parlour, and planted the Mole in an arm-chair in front of it, having fetched down a dressing-gown and slippers for him, and told him river stories till supper-time. Very thrilling stories they were, too, to an earth-dwelling animal like Mole. Stories about weirs, and sudden floods, and leaping pike, and steamers that flung hard bottles — at least bottles were certainly flung, and *from* steamers, so presumably *by* them; and about herons, and how particular they were whom they spoke to; and about adventures down drains, and night-fishings with Otter, or excursions far afield with Badger. Supper was a most cheerful meal; but very shortly afterwards a terribly sleepy Mole had to be escorted upstairs by his considerate host, to the best bedroom, where he soon laid his head on his pillow in great peace and contentment, knowing that his new-found friend the River was lapping the sill of his window.

This day was only the first of many similar ones for the emancipated Mole, each of them longer and fuller of interest as the ripening summer moved onward. He learnt to swim and to row and entered into the joy of running water; and with his ear to the reed-stems he caught, at intervals, something of what the wind went whispering so constantly among them.

Section Two
ALL AT SEA

ADVENTURES
UNDER FULL SAIL

from

THE TRUE CONFESSIONS OF CHARLOTTE DOYLE

PART I   by Avi

I awoke the next morning in my narrow bed — fully clothed — and a stark truth came to me. I was where no proper young lady should be. I needed only to close my eyes again to hear my father use those very words.

But as I lay there, feeling the same tossing motion I'd felt when falling asleep — I took it to be that of a ship moored to the dock — I recollected Mr Keetch saying that the *Seahawk* was due to leave by the morning's first tide. It was not too late. I would ask to be put ashore, and in some fashion — I hardly cared how — I'd make my way back to the Barrington School. There, with Miss Weed, I would be safe. She would make the necessary decisions.

Having composed my mind I sat up with some energy only to strike my head upon the low ceiling. Chastened, I got myself to the cabin floor. Now I discovered that my legs had become so weak, so rubbery, I all but sank to my knees. Still, my desperation was such that nothing could stop me. Holding on to now one part of the wall, now another, I made my way out of the cabin into the dim, close steerage and up the steps to the waist of the ship, only to receive the shock of my life.

Everywhere I looked great canvas sails of grey, from mainsail to main royal, from flying jib to trysail, were bellied out. Beyond the sails stretched the sky itself, as blue as a baby's bluest eyes, while the greenish sea, crowned with lacy caps of foaming white, rushed by with unrelenting speed. The *Seahawk* had gone to sea. We must have left Liverpool hours before!

As this realisation took hold, the *Seahawk*, almost as if wishing to offer final proof, pitched and rolled. Nausea choked me. My head pounded.

Weaker than ever, I turned around in search of support. For a fleeting but horrible second I had the notion that I was alone on board. Then I realised that I was being watched with crude curiosity. Standing on the quarter-deck was a red-faced man whose slight stoop and powerful broad shoulders conspired to give the impression of perpetual suspicion, an effect heightened by dark, deep-set eyes partially obscured by craggy eyebrows.

'Sir...' I called weakly. 'Where are we?'

'We're coasting down the Irish Sea, Miss Doyle,' replied the man, his voice raspy.

'I... I... I shouldn't be here,' I managed. But the man, seemingly indifferent to my words, only turned and with a slab of a hand reached for a bell set up at the head of the quarter-deck in a kind of gallows. He pulled the clapper three times. Even as I tried to keep myself from sinking to the deck nine men suddenly appeared in the ship's waist, from above as well as below, fore as well as aft. All wore the distinctive sailor's garb of canvas britches and shirts. A few had boots, while some had no shoes at all. One or two wore tarcovered hats, others caps of red cloth. Two had beards. One man had long hair and a ring in his left ear. Their faces were dark from sun and tar.

They were, in all, as sorry a group of men as I had ever seen: glum in expression, defeated in posture, with no character in any eye save sullenness. They were like men recruited from the doormat of Hell.

from

KON TIKI AND I

by Erik Hesselberg

*In 1947, six men set sail in a tiny bamboo raft to cross
the Pacific Ocean. Their voyage took 101 days.*

I

It was a strange sensation to see the tug disappear and to think of the enormous distance we were to drift on our little raft — a distance of open sea as far from Newcastle to the North Pole and back again to Newcastle. And far, far out to sea, 4300 sea miles away, we were to strike a few small islands, as small as grains of sand — in a craft without steering gear.

These thoughts came and went through my head the first night on the real sea, while the Kon-Tiki tossed up and down, up and down. The next log, on which Bengt lay, behaved differently.

But on the morning watch it was fresh and fine. A feeling that we were beginning a new life filled us — a life shared with the sea.

Then we saw two cockroaches on the logs and sympathised with them. They were in the same situation as we were but involuntarily. We called one Per and the other Lise.

Per was an unlucky fellow and tumbled overboard pretty soon. But Lise was with us almost the whole way to Polynesia, till she perished in the same tragic manner. Our other fellow-passengers — besides the parrot Lorita — were *ca*. 1000 ants. They lived in a cross-beam under my pillow. And a few thousand shell-fish held on to the logs in the cellar with the help of their suckers.

II

Fish were already jumping high round the vessel on our first days in the Humboldt Current. But soon we had something else to think about. For a time the wind and sea pretended not to see the curious insect. They left the impudent creature to the mercy of the current, which does not care if one is a splinter or a big steamer. But then they perceived that the insect was in earnest. And so they set to work to shake it off.

The third night was the worst — then there was a struggle for life on the logs. The seas hurled themselves over the stern to smash the steering oar and carry away the two men who were on watch there. The steering oar of tough wood, as hard as iron, cracked, but nothing much more happened. Our raft behaved well. The water poured over it continually, but that did not matter, for there were holes in the bottom so that it ran out again just as quickly. The logs creaked and twisted each in its own way. The cabin swayed in one direction and the mast in another, rather as if the whole show were made of India-rubber. But the lashings held well. The bad weather had more effect on us. Our bodies ached and we got little sleep. Knut lay flat and green with seasickness.

Afterwards no one felt so much as a qualm. All things have an end — and so the dirty water stopped being dirty and we felt we had everything very shipshape and pleasant.

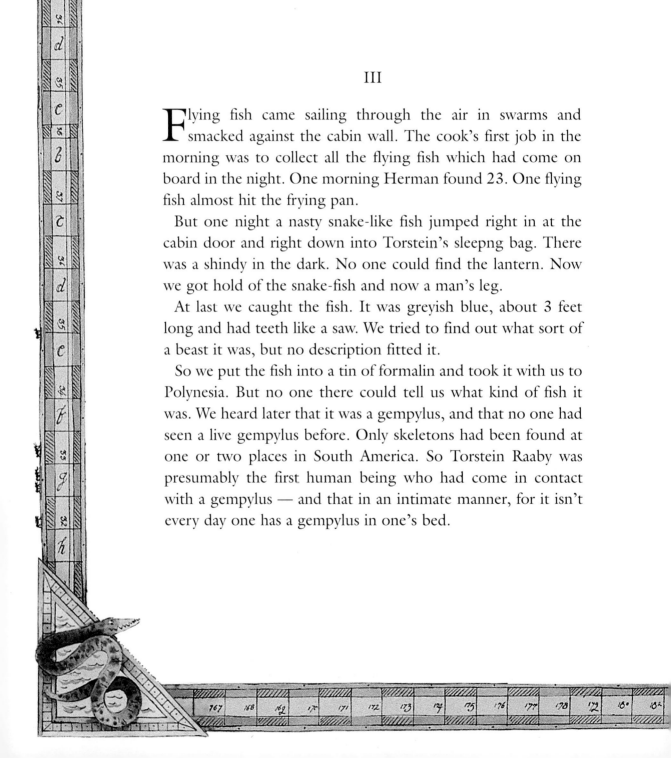

III

Flying fish came sailing through the air in swarms and smacked against the cabin wall. The cook's first job in the morning was to collect all the flying fish which had come on board in the night. One morning Herman found 23. One flying fish almost hit the frying pan.

But one night a nasty snake-like fish jumped right in at the cabin door and right down into Torstein's sleepng bag. There was a shindy in the dark. No one could find the lantern. Now we got hold of the snake-fish and now a man's leg.

At last we caught the fish. It was greyish blue, about 3 feet long and had teeth like a saw. We tried to find out what sort of a beast it was, but no description fitted it.

So we put the fish into a tin of formalin and took it with us to Polynesia. But no one there could tell us what kind of fish it was. We heard later that it was a gempylus, and that no one had seen a live gempylus before. Only skeletons had been found at one or two places in South America. So Torstein Raaby was presumably the first human being who had come in contact with a gempylus — and that in an intimate manner, for it isn't every day one has a gempylus in one's bed.

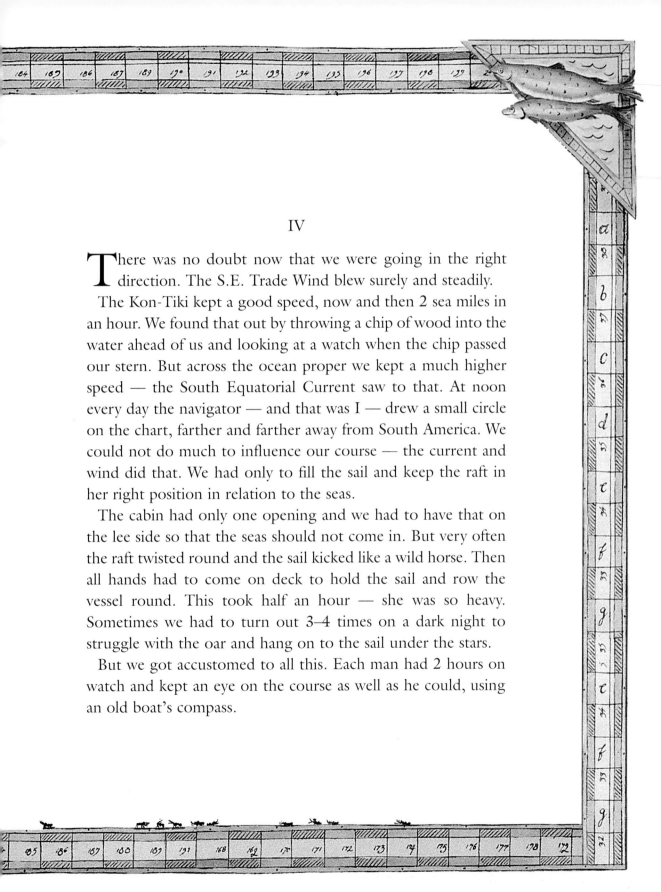

IV

There was no doubt now that we were going in the right direction. The S.E. Trade Wind blew surely and steadily.

The Kon-Tiki kept a good speed, now and then 2 sea miles in an hour. We found that out by throwing a chip of wood into the water ahead of us and looking at a watch when the chip passed our stern. But across the ocean proper we kept a much higher speed — the South Equatorial Current saw to that. At noon every day the navigator — and that was I — drew a small circle on the chart, farther and farther away from South America. We could not do much to influence our course — the current and wind did that. We had only to fill the sail and keep the raft in her right position in relation to the seas.

The cabin had only one opening and we had to have that on the lee side so that the seas should not come in. But very often the raft twisted round and the sail kicked like a wild horse. Then all hands had to come on deck to hold the sail and row the vessel round. This took half an hour — she was so heavy. Sometimes we had to turn out 3–4 times on a dark night to struggle with the oar and hang on to the sail under the stars.

But we got accustomed to all this. Each man had 2 hours on watch and kept an eye on the course as well as he could, using an old boat's compass.

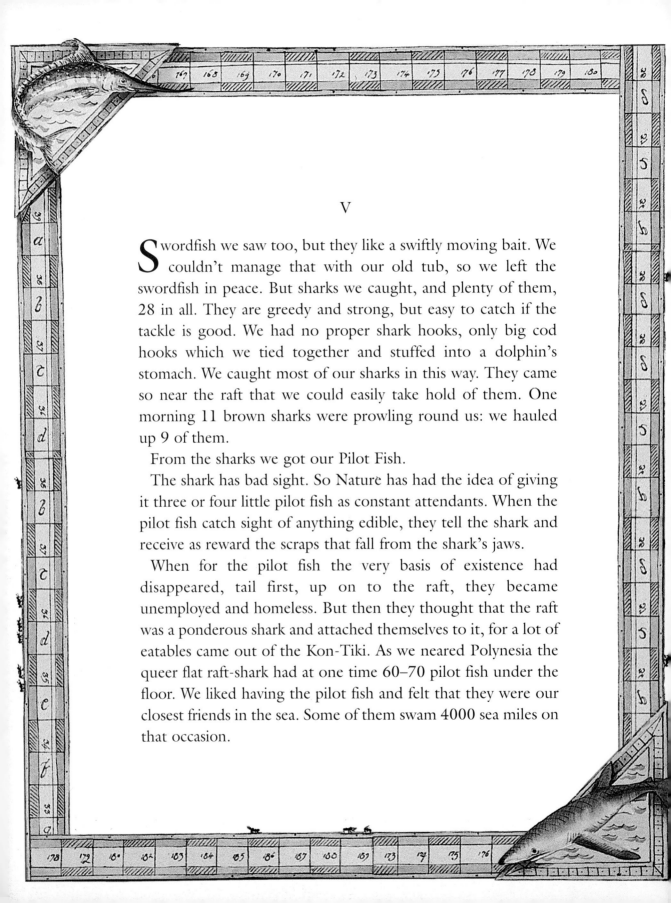

V

Swordfish we saw too, but they like a swiftly moving bait. We couldn't manage that with our old tub, so we left the swordfish in peace. But sharks we caught, and plenty of them, 28 in all. They are greedy and strong, but easy to catch if the tackle is good. We had no proper shark hooks, only big cod hooks which we tied together and stuffed into a dolphin's stomach. We caught most of our sharks in this way. They came so near the raft that we could easily take hold of them. One morning 11 brown sharks were prowling round us: we hauled up 9 of them.

From the sharks we got our Pilot Fish.

The shark has bad sight. So Nature has had the idea of giving it three or four little pilot fish as constant attendants. When the pilot fish catch sight of anything edible, they tell the shark and receive as reward the scraps that fall from the shark's jaws.

When for the pilot fish the very basis of existence had disappeared, tail first, up on to the raft, they became unemployed and homeless. But then they thought that the raft was a ponderous shark and attached themselves to it, for a lot of eatables came out of the Kon-Tiki. As we neared Polynesia the queer flat raft-shark had at one time 60–70 pilot fish under the floor. We liked having the pilot fish and felt that they were our closest friends in the sea. Some of them swam 4000 sea miles on that occasion.

O To Sail

by Walt Whitman

O to sail in a ship,
To leave this steady unendurable land,
To leave the tiresome sameness of the
  streets, the sidewalks and the houses,
To leave you, O you solid motionless
  land, and entering a ship,
To sail and sail and sail!

from

THE TRUE CONFESSIONS OF CHARLOTTE DOYLE
by Avi

PART II

For a second time I stood in the forecastle. The room was as dark and mean as when I'd first seen it. Now, however, I stood as a petitioner in sailor's garb. A glum Fisk was at my side. It hadn't been easy to convince him I was in earnest about becoming one of the crew. Even when he begrudged a willingness to believe in my sincerity he warned that agreement from the rest of the men would be improbable. He insisted I lay the matter before them immediately.

So it was that three men from Mr Hollybrass's watch, Grimes, Dillingham, and Foley, were the next to hear my plea. As Fisk had foretold, they were contemplating me and my proposal with very little evidence of favour.

'I do mean it,' I said, finding boldness with repetition, 'I want to be the replacement for Mr Johnson.'

'You're a girl,' Dillingham spat out contemptuously.

'A *pretty* girl,' Foley put in. It was not meant as a compliment. 'Takes more than canvas britches to hide that.'

'And a gentlewoman,' was Grimes's addition, as though that was the final evidence of my uselessness.

'I want to show that I stand with you,' I pleaded. 'That I made a mistake.'

'A mistake?' Foley snapped. 'Two able-bodied men have died!'

'Besides,' Dillingham agreed, 'you'll bring more trouble than good.'

'You can teach me,' I offered.

'God's fist,' Grimes cried. 'She thinks this is a school!'

'And the captain,' Foley asked. 'What'll he say?'

'He wants nothing more to do with me,' I replied.

'That's what he *says*. But you were his darling girl, Miss Doyle. We takes you in and he'll want you back again. Where will that put us?'

So it went, round and round. While the men made objections, while I struggled to answer them, Fisk said nothing.

Though I tried to keep my head up, my eyes steady, it was not easy. They looked at me as if I were some loathsome *thing*. At the same time, the more objections they made, the more determined I was to prove myself.

'See here, Miss Doyle,' Dillingham concluded, 'it's no simple matter. Understand, you sign on to the articles, so to speak, and you *are* on. No bolting to safe harbours at the first blow or when an ill word is flung your way. You're a hand or you're not a hand, and it won't go easy, that's all that can ever be promised.'

'I know,' I said.

'Hold out *your* hands,' he demanded.

Fisk nudged me. I held them out, palms up.

Foley peered over them. 'Like bloody cream,' he said with disgust. 'Touch mine!' he insisted and extended his. Gingerly, I touched one of them. His skin was like rough leather.

'That's the hands you'd get, miss. Like an animal. Is that what you want?'

'I don't care,' I said stoutly.

Finally it was Dillingham who said, 'And are you willing to take your place in the rigging too? Fair weather or foul?'

That made me pause.

Fisk caught the hesitation. 'Answer,' he prompted.

'Yes,' I said boldly.

They exchanged glances. Then Foley asked, 'What do the others think?'

Fisk shook his head and sighed. 'No doubt they'll speak the same.'

Suddenly Grimes said, 'Here's what I say: let her climb the royal yard. If she does it and comes down whole, and *still* is willing to serve, then I say let her sign and be bloody damned like the rest of us.'

'And do whatever she's called on to do!'

'No less!'

With no more than grunts the men seemed to agree among themselves. They turned towards me.

'*Now* what does Miss Doyle say?' Grimes demanded.

I swallowed hard, but all the same I gave yet another 'Yes'.

Foley came to his feet. 'All right then. I'll go caucus the others.' Out he went.

Fisk and I retreated to the galley while I waited for word. During that time he questioned me regarding my determination.

'Miss Doyle,' he pressed, 'you have agreed to climb to the top of the royal yard. Do you know that's the highest sail on the main mast? One hundred and thirty feet up. You can reach it only two ways. You can shimmy up the mast itself. Or you can climb the shrouds, using the ratlines for your ladder.'

I nodded as if I fully grasped what he was saying. The truth was that I didn't even wish to listen. I just wanted to get past the test.

'And, Miss Doyle,' he went on, 'if you slip and fall you'll be lucky to fall into the sea and drown quickly. No mortal could pluck you out fast enough to save you. Do you understand that?'

I swallowed hard but nodded. 'Yes.'

'Because if you're *not* lucky you'll crash to the deck. Fall that way and you'll either maim or kill yourself by breaking your neck. Still certain?'

'Yes,' I repeated, though somewhat more softly.

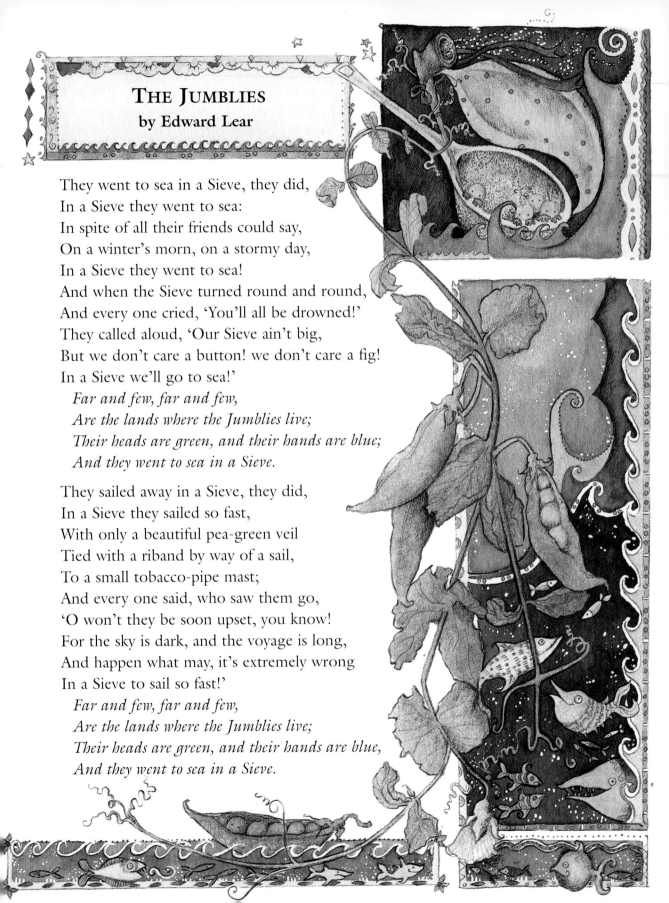

THE JUMBLIES
by Edward Lear

They went to sea in a Sieve, they did,
In a Sieve they went to sea:
In spite of all their friends could say,
On a winter's morn, on a stormy day,
In a Sieve they went to sea!
And when the Sieve turned round and round,
And every one cried, 'You'll all be drowned!'
They called aloud, 'Our Sieve ain't big,
But we don't care a button! we don't care a fig!
In a Sieve we'll go to sea!'
  Far and few, far and few,
  Are the lands where the Jumblies live;
  Their heads are green, and their hands are blue;
  And they went to sea in a Sieve.

They sailed away in a Sieve, they did,
In a Sieve they sailed so fast,
With only a beautiful pea-green veil
Tied with a riband by way of a sail,
To a small tobacco-pipe mast;
And every one said, who saw them go,
'O won't they be soon upset, you know!
For the sky is dark, and the voyage is long,
And happen what may, it's extremely wrong
In a Sieve to sail so fast!'
  Far and few, far and few,
  Are the lands where the Jumblies live;
  Their heads are green, and their hands are blue,
  And they went to sea in a Sieve.

The water it soon came in, it did,
The water it soon came in;
So to keep them dry, they wrapped their feet
In a pinky paper all folded neat,
And they fastened it down with a pin.
And they passed the night in a crockery-jar,
And each of them said, 'How wise we are!
Though the sky be dark, and the voyage be long,
Yet we never can think we were rash or wrong,
While round in our Sieve we spin!'
  Far and few, far and few,
  Are the lands where the Jumblies live;
  Their heads are green, and their hands are blue,
  And they went to sea in a Sieve.

And all night long they sailed away;
And when the sun went down,
They whistled and warbled a moony song
To the echoing sound of a coppery gong,
In the shade of the mountains brown.
'O Timballo! How happy we are,
When we live in a sieve and a crockery-jar,
And all night long in the moonlight pale,
We sail away with a pea-green sail,
In the shade of the mountains brown!'
  Far and few, far and few,
  Are the lands where the Jumblies live;
  Their heads are green, and their hands are blue,
  And they went to sea in a Sieve.

They sailed to the Western Sea, they did,
To a land all covered with trees,
And they bought an Owl, and a useful Cart,
And a pound of Rice, and a Cranberry Tart,
And a hive of silvery Bees.
And they bought a Pig, and some green Jack-daws,
And a lovely Monkey with lollipop paws,
And forty bottles of Ring-Bo-Ree,
And no end of Stilton Cheese.
  Far and few, far and few,
  Are the lands where the Jumblies live;
  Their heads are green, and their hands are blue,
  And they went to sea in a Sieve.

And in twenty years they all came back,
In twenty years or more,
And every one said, 'How tall they've grown!
For they've been to the Lakes, and the
  Torrible Zone,
And the hills of the Chankly Bore;
And they drank their health, and gave them a feast
Of dumplings made of beautiful yeast;
And every one said, 'If we only live,
We too will go to sea in a Sieve, —
To the hills of the Chankly Bore!'
  Far and few, far and few,
  Are the lands where the Jumblies live;
  Their heads are green, and their hands are blue,
  And they went to sea in a Sieve.

from

WE DIDN'T MEAN TO GO TO SEA

by Arthur Ransome

The wind was much stronger than it had been. Ripples had turned to waves, and every now and then the top of a wave turned to a splash of white foam as it came out of sight of the fog, lifted the stern of the *Goblin* and passed on.

'Look here, Susan,' said John. 'We can't go on like this. We must be close to the lightship and there's another lot of shoals beyond it. You take the tiller while I go down and have another look at that chart. But whatever you do, don't have a jibe. The wind's pretty well dead aft, and it's jolly hard not to. Come this side so that you can see the compass.'

Susan took the tiller. John pointed through the porthole at the compass card. 'Practically north-east... Keep it as near that as you can... But do look out for a jibe...'

Susan watched the card. If only it would keep still with the point marked N.E. against the thin black lubberline in the compass bowl. Too far one way... Now too far the other.

The mainsheet suddenly slackened. The sail flapped. The boom began to swing inboard. John put a quick hand on the tiller. The boom swung out once more and the sheet tautened with a jerk.

'Only just in time,' said John. 'You have to be awfully careful.'

'You keep the tiller,' said Susan with a gulp. 'I'll go down and get the chart.'

She climbed down the steep steps into the cabin. She had hardly got both feet on the cabin floor and a hand on the table to steady herself when she found herself swallowing hard though she had had nothing to drink. There seemed to be no air down here... none at all. It could not be that she was going to be sea-sick... yet... she found her mouth open... Air... That was what she wanted... She looked up at the fog through the companion-way... She saw John's head and shoulders, leaning forward, swinging this way and that against the dim grey background... If only

44

the cabin floor was not jerking about under her feet... She slipped and sat down on a bunk... Worse than ever... She clawed herself upright with the help of the table that was fixed to the floor but seemed to be trying to escape. Quick. Quick. Another minute down here and anything might happen. Where was that chart? It had slipped off the table and under it. She grovelled for it, grabbed it, flung herself at the steps and climbed out...

'I say, you haven't hurt yourself?' said Titty.

'I'm all right,' said Susan, swallowing fast and taking deep breaths of fog. Already she felt better. Perhaps it had been another false alarm. But even to look down those steps into the deep little cabin made her feel funny again. She must not look down there. She must look ahead, out into the fog... Buoys... lightship... Who would look after the others if anything were to go wrong with her?

She heard John talking. It was as if he were talking from far away. Perhaps he had already been talking for some time. What was he saying? No... No... He couldn't mean it...

'Shoals the other side of the lightship... lots of them... And shoals inshore... And that big lot where Jim said all those yachts had been wrecked must be somewhere over there.' He was pointing into the fog. 'But there's a clear way out between them. It's wide enough for anything, so long as we don't get too far north first...'

'But we can't... We can't.' Susan was again very near to tears.

'We've got to get outside the shoals,' said John. 'It isn't safe not to. Just look at the chart for yourself...'

Susan stared at the chart. It flapped in the wind as she held it. She stared at it, but it was as if she were looking at a blank sheet of paper. Her eyes simply would not work. What was it John wanted to do? Where did he say they were? John was talking still, almost as if he were arguing with himself, not with her. And then that foghorn blared again, close beside her.

'Oh, shut up, Roger!' she cried.

'I must do it twice more,' said Roger, 'or they'll think we're close-hauled.'

'Who'll think?'

'Anybody who hears it,' shouted Roger, as he pressed down the handle and the foghorn blared again.

'Only once more,' he said apologetically, hauling out the handle. 'This is the last of the three.'

Susan pushed the chart at John and put her hands to her ears.

John was still talking when she was able to listen to him again. 'We can't stop,' he was saying. 'Even if we had no sails, the tide would be taking us somewhere. You saw how it rushed us past those buoys. If it took us on a shoal, we'd be wrecked before we could do anything at all. And if we go on past the lightship we'll be charging into shoals on the other side of it. Remember what Jim said about that man who lost his boat. When in doubt keep clear of shoals. Get out to sea and stay there. If he were on board he'd be doing it now. He'd get outside as soon as he could and wait till he could see before trying to come back. And if we steer a bit south of east... Do look at the chart and you'll see...'

'But you don't know where we are now...'

'Yes I do. We must be getting near the lightship. Listen to it.'

'Beu .. eueueueueueu...'

'But we can't...'

'It's the only thing we can do,' said John.

'But we promised not to go to sea at all...' Susan moaned and turned her head away. Titty and Roger were both looking at her, and she could not bear to see their questioning faces.

'We didn't do it on purpose,' said John. 'We're at sea now, and we can't get back in the fog. If we tried we'd be bound to wreck the *Goblin* on something. Like trying to get through a narrow door in pitch dark. The door's wide open if we go the other way. You can see it yourself. If we go a bit east of south-east we'll get through. There's nothing for us to hit for miles. It's no good thinking of doing anything else. We've got to do it. South-east and a little bit east... and we'll be all right. But we've got to do it now or it'll be too late. That lightship's awfully near...'

'Beu... eueueueueueu...'

The Cork lightship, sending its bleat out into the fog once every fifteen seconds, was like the ticking of an enormous clock telling them they could not put things off for ever.

'We can't keep a promise when it's already broken,' said Titty.

'Is that another buoy' said John. 'Over there. Do keep a look out. I've got to watch the compass and the sail...'

'Can I sound the foghorn again?' said Roger.

'No... Wait half a minute. We've got to make up our minds.'

'Let's do what John says,' said Titty. 'Daddy'd say the same... You know... When it's Life and Death all rules go by the board. Of course, it isn't Life and Death yet, but it easily might be if we bumped the *Goblin* on a shoal.'

'How shall we ever get back?' said Susan.

'If we keep her going about south-east till the fog clears, we'll be able to get her back by turning round and coming north-west... And anyway, when it clears we'll be able to see things...'

'Beu... eueueueueueueu.'

The lightship bleated again and John's decision was made. There was not a moment to lose.

'I'm going to take her right out,' he said. 'Come on, Susan. We'll have to jibe. It'll be easier steering too. Come on. Will you take the tiller or shall I? You'd better. Bring her round when I say. Got to get the mainsheet in first. And there'll be the backstay to set up and the other one to cast off before the boom comes over. Titty... You be ready to let it go... Come on, Susan...'

'What about the jib?' said Roger. 'Shall I?...'

'Never mind about the jib till afterwards... So long as we get the boom over all right... Ready, Susan?'

Susan found herself at the tiller... found herself watching the burgee away up there in the fog as she had often watched the flag at the masthead of the tiny *Swallow* away on the lake in the north. John was hauling in the mainsheet, hand over hand, as fast as he could.

'Not yet, Susan... Not yet... Don't let her come yet... Help her, Roger... Just while I make fast.' He took a turn with the sheet and made ready to set up the backstay. The cockpit seemed full of ropes.

'Now then. Let go, Titty. Go on, Susan. Bring her round. Put your weight on the tiller, Roger. Good. She's coming... Now...'

The boom swung suddenly over their heads but John had hauled it so far in that it had not far to go. It brought up with a jerk not half as bad as he had expected. The *Goblin* heeled over to port. John had his backstay fast and was letting out the mainsheet a good deal quicker than he had been able to haul it in.

'Steady her,' he shouted. 'Don't let her come right round.'

Susan and Roger wrestled with the tiller.

'Oh look out... Don't let her jibe back again.'

'You take her,' begged Susan.

John, out of breath, took the tiller once more.

'We can let the jib come across now. Yes. Let go the sheet.'

The jib blew across the moment it was free. It hardly had time to flap before Susan had hauled in the port jibsheet and tamed it to quiet.

John, with two hands on the tiller, peered through the porthole at the swinging compass card. South, south-east... south-east... south-east by east... He must keep her heading like that. Easier now, with the wind on her quarter. No need to be afraid of a jibe, with all its dangers of breaking boom or backstay or even bringing down the mast in ruin. And even if the sails were not set as well as Jim would have set them, the *Goblin* was going beautifully. The chart, in the turmoil of jibing and changing course, had slipped to the floor of the cockpit. He picked it up from under his feet and looked at it, and then at the compass again. Gosh! Already pointing too far south. He pressed on the tiller and the compass card swung back to its old position and a little beyond it. Back again. He leaned on the tiller and tried to see both chart and compass at once. Yes, it must be all right. Clear water all the way till you came to the Sunk lightship right on the edge of the chart. Out there they would be alright. Jim had waited out there himself. This was what Jim would do. This was what Daddy would do. John, in spite of being able to see nothing but fog, in spite of the broken promise, in spite of the awful mess they were in, was surprised to find that a lot of his worry had left him. The decision had been made. He was dead sure it was the right decision. Sooner or later the fog would clear and he would have to think about getting back. Now the only thing to do was to steer a straight course, not to hit anything, to go on and on till he was clear of those awful shoals that were waiting to catch his blindfold little ship. John, in spite of his troubles, was for the moment almost happy.

THE TRUE CONFESSIONS OF CHARLOTTE DOYLE

by Avi

PART III

I will confess it, at that moment my nerves failed. I found myself unable to move. With thudding heart I looked frantically around. The members of the crew, arranged in a crescent, were standing like death's own jury.

It was Barlow who called out, 'A blessing goes with you, Miss Doyle.'

To which Ewing added, 'And this advice, Miss Doyle. Keep your eyes steady on the ropes. Don't you look down. Or up.'

For the first time I sensed that some of them at least wanted me to succeed. The realisation gave me courage.

With halting steps and shallow breath, I approached the rail only to pause when I reached it. I could hear a small inner voice crying, 'Don't! Don't!'

But it was also then that I heard Dillingham snicker, 'She'll not have the stomach.'

I reached up, grasped the lowest deadeye, and hauled myself atop the rail. That much I had done before. Now, I manoeuvred to the outside so that I would be leaning *into* the rigging and could even rest on it.

Once again I looked at the crew, *down* at them, I should say. They were staring up with blank expressions.

Recollecting Ewing's advice, I shifted my eyes and focused them on the ropes before me. Then, reaching as high as I could into one of the middle shrouds, and grabbing a ratline, I began to climb.

The ratlines were set about sixteen inches one above the other, so that the steps I had to take were wide for me. I needed to pull as much with arms as climb with legs. But line by line I did go up, as if ascending an enormous ladder.

After I had risen some seventeen feet I realised I'd made a great mistake. The rigging stood in sets, each going to a different level of the mast. I could have taken one that stretched directly to the top. Instead, I had chosen a line which went only to the first trestletree, to the top of the lower mast.

For a moment I considered backing down and starting afresh. I stole a quick glance below. The crew's faces were turned up toward me. I understood that they would take the smallest movement down as retreat. I had to continue.

And so I did.

Now I was climbing inside the lank grey-white sails, ascending, as it were, into a bank of dead clouds.

Beyond the sails lay the sea, slate-grey and ever rolling. Though the water looked calm, I could feel the slow pitch and roll it caused in the ship. I realised suddenly how much harder this climb would be if the wind were blowing and we were well under way. The mere thought made the palms of my hands grow damp.

Up I continued till I reached the main yard. Here I snatched another glance at the sea, and was startled to see how much bigger it had grown. Indeed, the more I saw of it the *more* there was. In contrast, the *Seahawk* struck me as having suddenly grown smaller. The more I saw of *her*, the *less* she was!

I glanced aloft. To climb higher I now had to edge myself out upon the trestletree and then once again move up the next set of ratlines as I'd done before. But at twice the height!

Wrapping one arm around the mast — even up here it was too big to reach around completely — I grasped one of the stays and edged out. At the same moment the ship dipped, the world seemed to twist and tilt down. My stomach lurched. My heart pounded. My head swam. In spite of myself I closed my eyes. I all but slipped, saving myself only by a sudden grasp of a line before the ship yawed the opposite way. I felt sicker yet. With ever-waning strength I clung on for dearest life. Now the full folly of what I was attempting burst upon me with grotesque reality. It had been not only stupid, but suicidal. I would never come down alive!

And yet I had to climb. This was my restitution.

When the ship was steady again, I grasped the furthest rigging, first with one hand, then the other, and dragged myself higher. I was heading for the topsail, fifteen feet further up.

Pressing myself as close as possible into the rigging, I continued to strain upward, squeezing the ropes so tightly my hands cramped. I even tried curling my toes about the ratlines.

At last I reached the topsail spar,
but discovered it was impossible to rest there. The only place
to pause was three *times* higher than the distance I'd just come, at the
trestletree just below the topgallant spar.

By now every muscle in my body ached. My head felt light, my heart
an anvil. My hands were on fire, the soles of my feet raw. Time and again
I was forced to halt, pressing my face against the rigging with eyes
closed. Then, in spite of what I'd been warned not to do, I opened them
and peered down. The *Seahawk* was like a wooden toy. The sea looked
greater still.

I made myself glance up. Oh, so far to go! How I forced myself to
move I am not sure. But the thought of backing down now was just as
frightening. Knowing only that I could not stay still, I crept upward,
ratline by ratline, taking what seemed to be for ever with each rise until

I finally reached the level just below the topgallant spar.

A seasoned sailor would have needed two minutes to reach this point. I had needed thirty!

Though I felt the constant roll of the ship, I had to rest there. What seemed like little movement on deck became, up high, wild swings and turns through treacherous air.

I gagged, forced my stomach down, drew breath, and looked out. Though I didn't think it possible, the ocean appeared to have grown greater yet. And when I looked down, the upturned faces of the crew appeared like so many tiny bugs.

There were twenty-five or so more feet to climb. Once again I grasped the rigging and hauled myself up.

This final climb was torture. With every upward pull the swaying of the ship seemed to increase. Even when not moving myself, I was flying through the air in wild, wide gyrations. The horizon kept shifting, tilting, dropping. I was increasingly dizzy, nauseous, terrified, certain that with every next moment I would slip and fall to my death. I paused again and again, my eyes on the rigging inches from my face, gasping and praying as I had never prayed before. My one hope was that, nearer to heaven now, I could make my desperation heard!

Inch by inch I continued up. Half an inch! Quarter inches! But then at last with trembling fingers, I touched the spar of the royal yard. I had reached the top.

Once there I endeavoured to rest again. But there the metronome motion of the mast was at its most extreme, the *Seahawk* turning, tossing, swaying as if trying to shake me off — like a dog throwing droplets of water from its back. And when I looked beyond I saw a sea that was infinity itself, ready, eager to swallow me whole.

I had to get back down.

As hard as it was to climb up, it was, to my horror, harder returning. On the ascent I could see where I was going. Edging down I had to grope blindly with my feet. Sometimes I tried to look. But when I did the sight of the void below was so sickening, I was forced to close my eyes.

Each groping step downward was a nightmare. Most times my foot found only air. Then, as if to mock my terror, a small breeze at last sprang up. Sails began to fill and snap, puffing in and out, at times smothering me. The tossing of the ship grew — if that were possible — more extreme.

Down I crept, past the topgallant where I paused briefly on the trestletree, then down along the longest stretch, towards the mainyard. It was there I fell.

I was searching with my left foot for the next ratline. When I found a hold and started to put my weight upon it, my foot, slipping on the slick tar surface, shot forward. The suddenness of it made me lose my grip. I tumbled backward, but in such a way that my legs became entangled in the lines. There I hung, *head downward*.

I screamed, tried to grab something. But I couldn't. I clutched madly at nothing, till my hand brushed against a dangling rope. I grabbed for it, missed, and grabbed again. Using all my strength, I levered myself up and, wrapping my arms into the lines, made a veritable knot of myself, mast, and rigging. Oh, how I wept! my entire body shaking and trembling as though it would break apart.

When my breathing became somewhat normal, I managed to untangle first one arm, then my legs. I was free.

I continued down. By the time I reached the mainyard I was numb and whimpering again, tears coursing from my eyes.

I moved to the shrouds I'd climbed, and edged myself past the lowest of the sails.

As I emerged from under it, the crew gave out a great 'Huzzah!'

Oh, how my heart swelled with exaltation!

Section Three

LET NOT THE DEEP SWALLOW ME UP

STORM, SHIPWRECK
AND
SURVIVAL

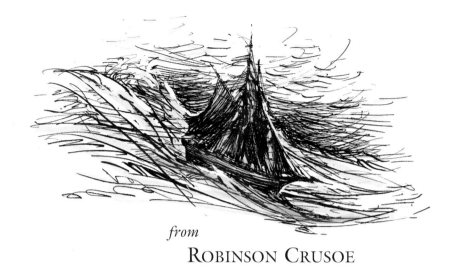

from

ROBINSON CRUSOE

PART I   by Daniel Defoe

It is not easy for any one, who has not been in the like condition, to describe or conceive the consternation of men in such circumstances; we knew nothing where we were, or upon what land it was we were driven, whether an island or the main, whether inhabited or not inhabited; and as the rage of the wind was still great, tho' rather less than at first, we could not so much as hope to have the ship hold many minutes without breaking in pieces, unless the winds by a kind of miracle should turn immediately about. In a word, we sat looking upon one another, and expecting death every moment, and every man acting accordingly, as preparing for another world, for there was little or nothing more for us to do in this; that which was our present comfort, and all the comfort we had was, that contrary to our expectation the ship did not break yet, and that the master said the wind began to abate.

Now tho' we thought that the wind did a little abate, yet the ship having thus struck upon the sand, and sticking too fast for us to expect her getting off, we were in a dreadful condition indeed, and had nothing to do but to think of saving our lives as well as we could; we had a boat at our stern just before the storm, but she was first stav'd by dashing against the ship's rudder, and in the next place she broke away, and either sunk or was driven off to sea, so there was no hope from her; we had another boat on board, but how to get her off into the sea was a doubtful thing; however, there was no room to debate, for we fancy'd the ship would break in pieces every minute, and some told us she was actually broken already.

In this distress the mate of our vessel lays hold of the boat, and with the help of the rest of the men, they got her slung over the ship's-side, and getting all into her, let go, and committed our selves, being eleven in number, to God's mercy and the wild sea; for tho' the storm was abated considerably, yet the sea went dreadful high upon the shore, and might well be call'd *den wild zee*, as the Dutch call the sea in a storm.

And now our case was very dismal indeed; for we all saw plainly, that the sea went so high that the boat could not live, and that we should be inevitably drowned. As to making sail, we had none, nor, if we had, could we ha' done any thing with it: so we work'd at the oar towards the land, tho' with heavy hearts, like men going to execution; for we all knew that when the boat came nearer the shore, she would be dash'd in a thousand pieces by the breach of the sea. However, we committed our souls to God in the most earnest manner, and the wind driving us towards the shore, we hasten'd our destruction with our own hands, pulling as well as we could towards land.

What the shore was, whether rock or sand, whether steep or shoal, we knew not; the only hope that could rationally give us the least shadow of expectation, was, if we might happen into some bay or gulph, or the mouth of some river, where by great chance we might have run our boat in, or got under the lee of the land, and perhaps made smooth water. But there was nothing of this appeared; but as we made nearer and nearer the shore, the land look'd more frightful than the sea.

After we had row'd, or rather driven, about a league and a half, as we reckon'd it, a raging wave, mountain-like, came rowling a-stern of us, and plainly bad us expect the *coup de grace*. In a word, it took us with such a fury, that it overset the boat at once; and separating us as well from the boat as from one another, gave us not time hardly to say, O God! for we were all swallowed up in a moment.

from

THE RIME OF THE ANCIENT MARINER

by Samuel Taylor Coleridge

'And now the STORM-BLAST came, and he
Was tyrannous and strong:
He struck with his o'ertaking wings,
And chased us south along.

With sloping masts and dipping prow,
As who pursued with yell and blow
Still treads the shadow of his foe,
And forward bends his head,
The ship drove fast, loud roared the blast,
And southward aye we fled.

And now there came both mist and snow,
And it grew wondrous cold:
And ice, mast-high, came floating by,
As green as emerald.

And through the drifts the snowy clifts
Did send a dismal sheen:
Nor shapes of men nor beasts we ken—
The ice was all between.
The ice was here, the ice was there,
The ice was all around:
It cracked and growled, and roared and howled,
Like noises in a swound!

At length did cross an Albatross,
Through the fog it came;
As if it had been a Christian soul,
We hailed it in God's name.

It ate the food it ne'er had eat,
And round and round it flew.
The ice did split with a thunder-fit;
The helmsman steered us through!

And a good south wind sprung up behind;
The Albatross did follow,
And every day, for food or play,
Came to the mariners' hollo!

In mist or cloud, on mast or shroud,
It perched for vespers nine;
Whiles all the night, through fog-smoke white,
Glimmered the white Moon-shine.'

'God save thee, ancient Mariner!
From the fiends that plague thee thus!—
Why look'st thou so?' — 'With my cross-bow
I shot the ALBATROSS.'

from

TWENTY THOUSAND LEAGUES UNDER THE SEA

by Jules Verne

The Nautilus, *a huge submarine, is cruising through the South Pole amidst treacherous icebergs.*

The next day, the 22nd of March, at six in the morning, preparations for departure were begun. The last gleams of twilight were melting into night. The cold was great; the constellations shone with wonderful intensity. In the zenith glittered that wondrous Southern Cross — the polar bear of antarctic regions. The thermometer showed twelve degrees below zero, and when the wind freshened, it was most biting. Flakes of ice increased on the open water. The sea seemed everywhere alike. Numerous blackish patches spread on the surface, showing the formation of fresh ice. Evidently the southern basin, frozen during the six winter months, was absolutely inaccessible. What became of the whales in that time? Doubtless they went beneath the icebergs, seeking more practicable seas. As to the seals and morses, accustomed to live in a hard climate, they remained on these icy shores. These creatures have the instinct to break holes in the ice-fields, and to keep them open. To these holes they come for breath; when the birds, driven away by the cold, have emigrated to the north, these sea-mammals remain sole masters of the polar continent. But the reservoirs were filling with water, and the *Nautilus* was slowly descending. At 1000 feet deep it stopped; its screw beat the waves, and it advanced straight towards the north, at a speed of fifteen miles an hour. Towards night it was already floating under the immense body of the iceberg. At three in the morning I was awakened by a violent shock. I sat up in my bed and listened in the darkness, when I was thrown into the middle of the room. The *Nautilus*, after having struck, had rebounded violently. I groped along the partition, and by the staircase to the saloon, which was lit by the luminous ceiling. The furniture was upset. Fortunately the windows were firmly set, and had held fast. The pictures on the starboard side, from being no longer vertical, were clinging to the paper, whilst those of the port side were hanging at least a foot from the wall. The *Nautilus* was lying on its starboard side perfectly motionless. I heard footsteps, and a confusion of voices; but Captain Nemo did not appear. As I was leaving the saloon, Ned Land and Conseil entered.

'What is the matter?' said I, at once.

'I came to ask you, sir,' replied Conseil.

'Confound it!' exclaimed the Canadian, 'I know well enough! The *Nautilus* has struck; and judging by the way she lies, I do not think she will right herself as she did the first time in Torres Straits.'

'But,' I asked, 'has she at least come to the surface of the sea?'

'We do not know,' said Conseil.

'It is easy to decide,' I answered. I consulted the manometer. To my great surprise it showed a depth of more than 180 fathoms. 'What does that mean?' I exclaimed.

'We must ask Captain Nemo,' said Conseil.

'But where shall we find him?' said Ned Land.

'Follow me,' said I, to my companions.

We left the saloon. There was no one in the library. At the centre staircase, by the berths of the ship's crew, there was no one. I thought that Captain Nemo must be in the pilot's cage. It was best to wait. We all returned to the saloon. For twenty minutes we remained thus, trying to hear the slightest noise which might be made on board the *Nautilus*, when Captain Nemo entered. He seemed not to see us; his face, generally so impassive, showed signs of uneasiness. He watched the compass silently, then the manometer and going to the planisphere, placed his finger on a spot representing the southern seas. I would not interrupt him; but, some minutes later, when he turned towards me, I said using one of his own expressions in the Torres Straits —

'An incident, Captain?'

'No, sir; an accident this time.'

'Serious?'

'Perhaps.'

'Is the danger immediate?'

'No.'

'The *Nautilus* has stranded?'

'Yes.'

'And this has happened — how?'

'From a caprice of nature, not from the ignorance of man. Not a mistake has been made in the working. But we cannot prevent equilibrium from producing its effects. We may brave human laws, but we cannot resist natural ones.'

Captain Nemo had chosen a strange moment for uttering this philosophical reflection. On the whole, his answer helped me little.

'May I ask, sir, the cause of this accident?'

'An enormous block of ice, a whole mountain, has turned over,' he replied. 'When icebergs are undermined at their base by warmer water or reiterated shocks, their centre of gravity rises, and the whole thing turns over. This is what has happened; one of these blocks, as it fell, struck the *Nautilus*, then, gliding under its hull, raised it with irresistible force, bringing it into beds which are not so thick, where it is lying on its side.'

'But can we not get the *Nautilus* off by emptying its reservoirs, that it may regain its equilibrium?'

'That, sir, is being done at this moment. You can hear the pump working. Look at the needle of the manometer; it shows that the *Nautilus* is rising, but the block of ice is rising with it; and, until some obstacle stops its ascending motion, our position cannot be altered.'

Indeed' the *Nautilus* still held the same position to starboard; doubtless it would right itself when the block stopped But at this moment who knows if we may not strike the upper part of the iceberg, and if we may not be frightfully crushed between the two glassy surfaces? I reflected on all the consequences of our position. Captain Nemo never took his eyes off the manometer. Since the fall of the iceberg, the *Nautilus* had risen about a hundred and fifty feet, but it still made the same angle with the perpendicular. Suddenly a slight movement was felt in the hold. Evidently it was righting a little. Things hanging in the saloon were sensibly returning to their normal position. The partitions were nearing the upright No one spoke. With beating hearts we watched and felt the straightening. The boards became horizontal under our feet. Ten minutes passed.

'At last we have righted!' I exclaimed.

'Yes,' said Captain Nemo, going to the door of the saloon.

'But are we floating?' I asked.

'Certainly,' he replied; 'since the reservoirs are not empty; and, when empty, the *Nautilus* must rise to the surface of the sea.'

We were in open sea; but at a distance of about ten yards, on either side of the *Nautilus*, rose a dazzling wall of ice. Above and beneath the same wall. Above, because the lower surface of the iceberg stretched over us like an immense ceiling. Beneath, because the overturned block, having slid by degrees, had found a resting-place on the lateral walk, which kept it in that position. The *Nautilus* was really imprisoned in a perfect tunnel of ice more than twenty yards in breadth, filled with quiet water. It was easy to get out of it by going either forward or backward, and then make a free passage under the iceberg, some hundreds of yards deeper. The luminous ceiling had been extinguished, but the saloon was still resplendent with intense light. It was the powerful reflection from the glass partition sent violently back to the sheets of the lantern. I cannot describe the effect of the voltaic rays upon the great blocks so capriciously cut; upon every angle, every ridge, every facet was thrown a different light, according to the nature of the veins running through the ice; a dazzling mine of gems, particularly of sapphires, their blue rays crossing with the green of the emerald. Here and there were opal shades of wonderful softness, running through bright spots like diamonds of fire, the brilliancy of which the eye could not bear. The power of the lantern seemed increased a hundredfold, like a lamp through the lenticular plates of a first-class lighthouse.

'How beautiful! How beautiful!' cried Conseil.

'Yes,' I said, 'it is a wonderful sight. Is it not, Ned?'

'Yes, confound it! Yes,' answered Ned Land, 'it is superb! I am mad at being obliged to admit it. No one has ever seen anything like it, but the sight may cost us dear. And if I must say all, I think we are seeing here things which God never intended man to see.'

Ned was right, it was too beautiful. Suddenly a cry from

Conseil made me turn.

'What is it?' I asked.

'Shut your eyes, sir! Do not look, sir!' Saying which, Conseil clapped his hands over his eyes.

'But what is the matter, my boy?'

'I am dazzled, blinded.'

My eyes turned involuntarily towards the glass, but I could not stand the fire which seemed to devour them. I understood what had happened. The *Nautilus* had put on full speed. All the quiet lustre of the ice-walk was at once changed into flashes of lightning. The fire from these myriads of diamonds was blinding. It required some time to calm our troubled looks. At last the hands were taken down.

'Faith, I should never have believed it,' said Conseil.

It was then five in the morning; and at that moment a shock was felt at the bows of the *Nautilus*. I knew that its spur had struck a block of ice. It must have been a false manoeuvre, for this submarine tunnel, obstructed by blocks, was not very easy navigation. I thought that Captain Nemo, by changing his course, would either turn these obstacles, or else follow the windings of the tunnel. In any case, the road before us could not be entirely blocked. But, contrary to my expectations, the *Nautilus* took a decided retrograde motion.

'We are going backwards?' said Conseil

'Yes,' I replied 'This end of the tunnel can have no egress.'

'And then?'

'Then,' said I, 'the working is easy. We must go back again, and go out at the southern opening. That is all.'

In speaking thus, I wished to appear more confident than I really was. But the retrograde motion of the *Nautilus* was increasing; and, reversing the screw, it carried us at great speed.

'It will be a hindrance,' said Ned.

'What does it matter, some hours more or less, provided we get out at last?'

'Yes,' repeated Ned Land, 'provided we do get out at last!'

For a short time I walked from the saloon to the library. My companions were silent. I soon threw myself on an ottoman, and took a

book which my eyes overran mechanically. A quarter of an hour after, Conseil, approaching me, said, 'Is what you are reading very interesting, sir?'

'Very interesting!' I replied.

'I should think so, sir. It is your own book you are reading.'

'My book?'

And indeed I was holding in my hand the work on the 'Great Submarine Depths.' I did not even dream of it, I closed the book, and returned to my walk. Ned and Conseil rose to go.

'Stay here, my friends,' said I, detaining them. 'Let us remain together until we are out of this block.'

'As you please, sir,' Conseil replied.

Some hours passed. I often looked at the instruments hanging from the partition. The manometer showed that the *Nautilus* kept at a constant depth of more than three hundred yards; the compass still pointed to the south; the log indicated a speed of twenty miles an hour, which, in such a cramped space, was very great. But Captain Nemo knew that he could not hasten too much, and that minutes were worth ages to us. At twenty-five minutes past eight a second shock took place, this time from behind. I turned pale. My companions were close by my side. I seized Conseil's hand. Our looks expressed our feelings better than words. At this moment the Captain entered the saloon. I went up to him.

'Our course is barred southward?' I asked.

'Yes, sir. The iceberg has shifted, and closed every outlet'

'We are blocked up, then?'

'Yes.'

from

THE SWISS FAMILY ROBINSON

by J.D. Wyss

*Abandoned by the ship's crew, the family must
build a raft to flee the sinking ship.*

We very soon found four large casks, made of sound wood, and strongly bound with iron hoops; they were floating with many other things in the water in the hold, but we managed to fish them out, and drag them to a suitable place for launching them. They were exactly what I wanted, and I succeeded in sawing them across the middle. Hard work it was, and we were glad enough to stop and refresh ourselves with wine and biscuits.

My eight tubs now stood ranged in a row near the water's edge, and I looked at them with great satisfaction; to my surprise, my wife did not seem to share my pleasure!

'I shall never,' said she, 'muster courage to get into one of these!'

'Do not be too sure of that, dear wife; when you see my contrivance completed, you will perhaps prefer it to this immovable wreck.'

I next procured a long thin plank on which my tubs could be fixed, and the two ends of this I bent upwards so as to form a keel. Other two planks were nailed along the sides of the tubs; they also being flexible, were brought to a point at each end, and all firmly secured and nailed together. I felt satisfied that in smooth water this craft would be perfectly trustworthy. But when we thought all was ready for the launch, we found, to our dismay, that the grand contrivance was so heavy and clumsy, that even our united efforts could not move it an inch.

'I must have a lever,' cried I. 'Run and fetch the capstan bar!'

Fritz quickly brought one and, having formed rollers by cutting up a long spar, I raised the forepart of my boat with the bar, and my sons placed a roller under it.

'How is it, father,' inquired Ernest, 'that with that thing you alone can do more than all of us together?'

I explained, as well as I could in a hurry, the principle of the lever; and promised to have a long talk on the subject of Mechanics, should we have a future opportunity.

I now made fast a long rope to the stern of our boat, attaching the other end to a beam; then placing a second and third roller under it, we once more began to push, this time with success, and soon our gallant craft was safely launched: so swiftly indeed did she glide into the water that, but for the rope, she would have passed beyond our reach. The boys wished to jump in directly; but, alas, she leaned so much on one side that they could not venture to do so.

Some heavy things being thrown in, however, the boat righted itself by degrees, and the boys were so delighted that they struggled which should first leap in to have the fun of sitting down in the tubs. But it was plain to me at once that something more was required to make her perfectly safe, so I contrived outriggers to preserve the balance, by nailing long poles across at the stem and stern, and fixing at the ends of each empty brandy casks. Then the boat appearing steady, I got in; and turning it towards the most open side of the wreck, I cut and cleared away obstructions, so as to leave a free passage for our departure, and the boys brought oars to be ready for the voyage. This important undertaking we were forced to postpone until the next day, as it was by this time far too late to attempt it. It was not pleasant to have to spend another night in so precarious a situation; but, yielding to necessity, we sat down to enjoy a comfortable supper, for during our exciting and incessant work all day we had taken nothing but an occasional biscuit and a little wine.

We prepared for rest in a much happier frame of mind than on the preceding day, but I did not forget the possibility of a renewed storm, and therefore made every one put on the belts as before. Then retiring to our berths, peaceful sleep prepared us all for the exertions of the coming day.

We rose up betimes, for sleep weighs lightly on the hopeful, as well as on the anxious. After kneeling together in prayer, 'Now my beloved ones,' said I, 'with God's help we are about to effect our escape. Let the poor animals we must leave behind, be well fed, and put plenty of fodder within their reach: in a few days we may be able to return, and save them likewise. After that, collect everything you can think of which may be of use to us.'

The boys joyfully obeyed me, and I selected from the large quantity of stores they got together, canvas to make a tent, a chest of carpenter's tools, guns, pistols, powder, shot, and bullets, rods and fishing tackle, an iron pot, a case of portable soup and another of biscuit. These useful articles of course took the place of the ballast I had hastily thrown in the day before.

With a hearty prayer for God's blessing, we now began to take our seats, each in his tub. Just then we heard the cocks begin to crow, as though to reproach us for deserting them. 'Why should not the fowls go with us!' exclaimed I. 'If we find no food for *them*, they can be food for us!' Ten hens and a couple of cocks were accordingly placed in one of the tubs, and secured with some wire-netting over them.

The ducks and geese were set at liberty, and took to the water at once, while the pigeons, rejoicing to find themselves on the wing, swiftly made for the shore. My wife, who managed all this for me, kept us waiting for her some little time, and came at last with a bag as big as a pillow in her arms. 'This is *my* contribution,' said she, throwing the bag to little Franz, to be, as I thought, a cushion for him to sit upon.

All being ready, we cast off, and moved away from the wreck. My good, brave wife sat in the first compartment of the boat; next her was Franz, a pretty little boy, nearly eight years old. Then came Fritz, a handsome, spirited young fellow of fifteen; the two centre tubs contained the valuable cargo; then came our bold, thoughtless Jack; next him Ernest, my second son, intelligent, well-informed, and rather indolent. I myself, the anxious, loving father, stood in the stern, endeavouring to guide the raft with its precious burden to a safe landing-place.

The elder boys took the oars, everyone wore a float belt, and had something useful close to him in case of being thrown into the water.

The tide was flowing, which was a great help to the young oarsmen. We emerged from the wreck and glided into the open sea. All eyes were strained to get a full view of the land, and the boys pulled with a will; but for some time we made no progress, as the boat kept turning round and round, until I hit upon the right way to steer it, after which we merrily made for the shore.

We had left the two dogs, Turk and Juno, on the wreck, as being both large mastiffs we did not care to have their additional weight on board our craft; but when they saw us apparently deserting them, they set up a piteous howl, and sprang into the sea. I was sorry to see this, for the distance to the land was so great that I scarcely expected them to be able to accomplish it. They followed us, however, and, occasionally resting their fore-paws on the outriggers, kept up with us well. Jack was inclined to deny them this their only chance of safety. 'Stop,' said I, 'that would be unkind as well as foolish; remember, the merciful man regardeth the life of his beast.'

Our passage though tedious was safe; but the nearer we approached the shore the less inviting it appeared; the barren rocks seemed to threaten us with misery and want.

Many casks, boxes and bales of goods floated on the water around us. Fritz and I managed to secure a couple of hogsheads, so as to tow them alongside. With the prospect of famine before us, it was desirable to lay hold of anything likely to contain provisions.

By-and-by we began to perceive that, between and beyond the cliffs, green grass and trees were discernible. Fritz could distinguish many tall palms, and Ernest hoped they would prove to be coconut trees, and enjoyed the thoughts of drinking the refreshing milk.

'I am very sorry I never thought of bringing away the Captain's telescope,' said I.

'Oh, look here, father!' cried Jack, drawing a little spy-glass joyfully

out of his pocket.

By means of this glass, I made out that at some distance to the left the coast was much more inviting; a strong current however carried us directly towards the frowning rocks, but I presently observed an opening, where a stream flowed into the sea, and saw that our geese and ducks were swimming towards this place. I steered after them into the creek, and we found ourselves in a small bay or inlet where the water was perfectly smooth and of moderate depth. The ground sloped gently upwards from the low banks to the cliffs which here retired inland, leaving a small plain, on which it was easy for us to land. Everyone sprang gladly out of the boat but little Franz, who, lying packed in his tub like a potted shrimp, had to be lifted out by his mother.

The dogs had scrambled on shore before us; they received us with loud barking and the wildest demonstrations of delight. The geese and ducks kept up an incessant din, added to which was the screaming and croaking of flamingos and penguins, whose dominion we were invading. The noise was deafening, but far from unwelcome to me, as I thought of the good dinners the birds might furnish.

As soon as we could gather our children around us on dry land, we knelt to offer thanks and praise for our merciful escape, and with full hearts we commended ourselves to God's good keeping for the time to come.

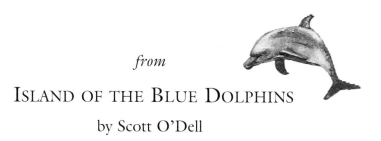

from

ISLAND OF THE BLUE DOLPHINS

by Scott O'Dell

A young girl, separated from her tribe, is left alone on a deserted island.

I had decided during the days of the storm, when I had given up hope of seeing the ship, that I would take one of the canoes and go to the country that lay towards the east. I remembered how Kimki, before he had gone, had asked the advice of his ancestors who had lived many ages in the past, who had come to the island from that country, and likewise the advice of Zuma, the medicine man who held power over the wind and the seas. But these things I could not do, for Zuma had been killed by the Aleuts, and in all my life I had never been able to speak with the dead, though many times I had tried.

Yet I cannot say that I was really afraid as I stood there on the shore. I knew that my ancestors had used the sea in their canoes, coming from that place which lay beyond. Kimki, too, had crossed the sea. I was not nearly so skilled with a canoe as these men, but I must say that whatever might befall me on the endless waters did not trouble me. It meant far less than the thought of staying on the island alone, without a home or companions, pursued by wild dogs, where everything reminded me of those who were dead and those who had gone away.

Of the four canoes stored there against the cliff, I chose the smallest, which was still very heavy because it could carry six people. The task that faced me was to push it down the rocky shore and into the water, a distance four or five times its length.

This I did by first removing all the large rocks in front of the canoe. I then filled in all these holes with pebbles and along this path laid down long strips of kelp, making a slippery bed. The shore was steep and once I got the canoe to move with its own weight, it slid down the path and into the water.

The sun was in the west when I left the shore. The sea was calm behind the high cliffs. Using the two-bladed paddle I quickly skirted the south part of the island. As I reached the sandspit the wind struck. I was paddling from the back of the canoe because you can go faster kneeling there, but I could not handle it in the wind.

Kneeling in the middle of the canoe, I paddled hard and did not pause until I had gone through the tides that run fast around the sandspit. There were many small waves and I was soon wet, but as I came out from behind the spit the spray lessened and the waves grew long and rolling. Though it would have been easier to go the way they slanted, this would have taken me in the wrong direction. I therefore kept them on my left hand, as well as the island, which grew smaller and smaller, behind me.

At dusk I looked back. The Island of the Blue Dolphins had disappeared. This was the first time that I felt afraid.

There were only hills and valleys of water around me now. When I was in a valley I could see nothing and when the canoe rose out of it, only the ocean stretching away and away.

Night fell and I drank from the basket. The water cooled my throat.

The sea was black and there was no difference between it and the sky. The waves made no sound among themselves, only faint noises as they went under the canoe or struck against it. Sometimes the noises seemed angry and at other times like people laughing. I was not hungry because of my fear.

The first star made me feel less afraid. It came out low in the sky and it was in front of me, towards the east. Other stars began to appear all around, but it was this one I kept my gaze upon. It was in the figure that we call a serpent, a star which shone green and which I knew. Now and then it was hidden by mist, yet it always came out brightly again.

Without this star I would have been lost, for the waves never changed. They came always from the same direction and in a manner that kept pushing me away from the place I wanted to reach. For this reason the canoe made a path in the black water like a snake. But somehow I kept moving towards the star which shone in the east.

This star rose high and then I kept the North Star on my left hand, the one we call 'the star that does not move'. The wind grew quiet. Since it always died down when the night was half over, I knew how long I had been travelling and how far away the dawn was.

About this time I found that the canoe was leaking. Before dark I had emptied one of the baskets in which food was stored and used it to dip out the water that came over the sides. The water that now moved around my knees was not from the waves.

I stopped paddling and worked with the basket until the bottom of the canoe was almost dry. Then I searched around, feeling in the dark along the smooth planks, and found the place near the bow where the water was seeping through a crack as long as my hand and the width of a finger. Most of the time it was out of the sea, but it leaked whenever the canoe dipped forward in the waves.

The places between the planks were filled with black pitch which we gather along the shore. Lacking this, I tore a piece of fibre from my skirt and pressed it into the crack, which held back the water.

Dawn broke in a clear sky and as the sun came out of the waves I saw that it was far off on my left. During the night I had drifted south of the place I wished to go, so I changed my direction and paddled along the path made by the rising sun.

There was no wind on this morning and the long waves went quietly under the canoe. I therefore moved faster than during the night.

I was very tired, but more hopeful than I had been since I left the island. If the good weather did not change I would cover many leagues before dark. Another night and another day might bring me within sight of the shore towards which I was going.

Not long after dawn, while I was thinking of this strange place and what it would look like, the canoe began to leak again. This crack was between the same planks, but was a larger one and close to where I was kneeling.

The fibre I tore from my skirt and pushed into the crack held back most of the water which seeped in whenever the canoe rose and fell with the waves. Yet I could see that the planks were weak from one end to the other, probably from the canoe being stored so long in the sun, and that they might open along their whole length if the waves grew rougher.

It was suddenly clear to me that it was dangerous to go on. The voyage would take two more days, perhaps longer. By turning back to the island

I would not have nearly so far to travel.

Still I could not make up my mind to do so. The sea was calm and I had come far. The thought of turning back after all this labour was more than I could bear. Even greater was the thought of the deserted island I would return to, of living there alone and forgotten. For how many suns and how many moons?

The canoe drifted idly on the calm sea while these thoughts went over and over in my mind, but when I saw the water seeping through the crack again, I picked up the paddle. There was no choice except to turn back towards the island.

I knew that only by the best of fortune would I ever reach it.

The wind did not blow until the sun was overhead. Before that time I covered a good distance, pausing only when it was necessary to dip water from the canoe. With the wind I went more slowly and had to stop more often because of the water spilling over the sides, but the leak did not grow worse.

This was my first good fortune. The next was when a swarm of dolphins appeared. They came swimming out of the west, but as they saw the canoe they turned around in a great circle and began to follow me. They swam up slowly and so close that I could see their eyes, which are large and the colour of the ocean. Then they swam on ahead of the canoe, crossing back and forth in front of it, diving in and out, as if they were weaving a piece of cloth with their broad snouts.

Dolphins are animals of good omen. It made me happy to have them swimming around the canoe, and though my hands had begun to bleed from the chafing of the paddle, just watching them made me forget the pain. I was very lonely before they appeared, but now I felt that I had friends with me and did not feel the same.

The blue dolphins left me shortly before dusk. They left as quickly as they had come, going on into the west, but for a long time I could see the last of the sun shining on them. After night fell I could still see them in my thoughts and it was because of this that I kept on paddling when I wanted to lie down and sleep.

More than anything, it was the blue dolphins that took me back home.

Fog came with the night, yet from time to time I could see the star that stands high in the west, the red star called Magat which is part of the figure that looks like a crawfish and is known by that name. The crack in the planks grew wider so I had to stop often to fill it with fibre and to dip out the water.

The night was very long, longer than the night before. Twice I dozed kneeling there in the canoe, though I was more afraid than I had ever been. But the morning broke clear and in front of me lay the dim line of the island like a great fish sunning itself on the sea.

I reached it before the sun was high, the sandspit and its tides that bore me into the shore. My legs were stiff from kneeling and as the canoe struck the sand I fell when I rose to climb out. I crawled through the shallow water and up the beach. There I lay for a long time, hugging the sand in happiness.

WHAT PAIN IT WAS TO DROWN

from Richard III

by William Shakespeare

O Lord, methought what pain it was to drown,
What dreadful noise of waters in mine ears,
What sights of ugly death within mine eyes!
Methought I saw a thousand fearful wrecks:
A thousand men that fishes gnawed upon,
Wedges of gold, great anchors, heaps of pearl,
Inestimable stones, unvalued jewels,
All scattered in the bottom of the sea:
Some lay in dead men's skulls, and in the holes
Where eyes did once inhabit, there were crept,
As 'twere in scorn of eyes, reflecting gems,
That wooed the slimy bottom of the deep,
And mocked the dead bones that lay scattered by.

from

ROBINSON CRUSOE

by Daniel Defoe

PART II

Nothing can describe the confusion of thought which I felt when I sunk into the water; for tho' I swam very well, yet I could not deliver my self from the waves so as to draw breath, till that wave having driven me, or rather carried me a vast way on towards the shore, and having spent itself, went back, and left me upon the land almost dry, but half-dead with the water I took in. I had so much presence of mind as well as breath left, that seeing my self nearer the main land than I expected, I got upon my feet, and endeavoured to make on towards the land as fast as I could, before another wave should return, and take the up again. But I soon found it was impossible to avoid it; for I saw the sea come after me as high as a great hill, and as furious as an enemy which I had no means or strength to contend with; my business was to hold my breath, and raise myself upon the water, if I could; and so by swimming to preserve my breathing, and pilot my self towards the shore, if possible; my greatest concern now being that the sea, as it would carry me a great way towards the shore when it came on, might not carry me back again with it when it gave back towards the sea.

The wave that came upon me again, buried me at once 20 or 30 foot deep in its own body; and I could feel my self carried with a mighty force and swiftness towards the shore a very great way; but I held my breath, and assisted my self to swim still forward with all my might. I was ready to burst with holding my breath, when, as I felt my self rising up, so to my immediate relief, I found my head and hands shoot out above the surface of the water; and tho' it was not two seconds of time that I could keep my self so, yet it reliev'd me greatly, gave me breath and new courage. I was covered again with water a good while, but not so long but I held it out; and finding the water had spent it self, and began to return, I strook forward against the return of the waves, and felt ground again with my feet. I stood still a few moments to recover breath, and till the water went from me, and then took to my heels, and run with what strength I had farther towards the shore. But neither would this deliver me from the fury of the sea, which came pouring in after me again, and twice more I was lifted up by the waves and carried forwards as before, the shore being very flat.

The last of these two had well near been fatal to me; for the sea having hurried me along as before, landed me, or rather dash'd me against a piece of rock, and that with such force as it left me senseless, and indeed helpless as to my own deliverance; for the blow taking my side and breast, beat the beat the breath as it were quite out of my body; and had it returned again immediately, I must have been strangled in the water; but I recover'd a little before the return of the waves, and seeing I should be cover'd again with the water, I resolv'd to hold fast by a piece of the rock, and so to hold my breath, if possible, till the wave went back; now as waves were not so high as at first, being nearer land, I held my hold till the wave abated, and then fetch'd another run, which brought me so near the shore, that the next wave, tho' it went over me, yet did not so swallow me up as to carry me away, and the next run I took, I got to the main land, where, to my great comfort, I clamber'd up the clifts of the shore and sat me down upon the grass, free from danger, and quite out of the reach of the water.

Section Four

THE TERROR
OF THE SEAS

PIRATES, MUTINY
AND
MURDER

from

THE ADVENTURES OF TOM SAWYER

PART I

by Mark Twain

Tom's mind was made up now. He was gloomy and desperate. He was a forsaken, friendless boy, he said; nobody loved him; when they found out what they had driven him to, perhaps they would be sorry; he had tried to do right and get along, but they would not let him; since nothing would do them but to be rid of him, let it be so; and let them blame him for the consequences — why shouldn't they? what right had the friendless to complain? Yes, they had forced him to it at last: he would lead a life of crime. There was no choice.

By this time he was far down Meadow Land, and the bell for school to 'take up' tinkled faintly upon his ear. He sobbed, now, to think he should never, never hear that old familiar sound any more — it was very hard, but it was forced on him; since he was driven out into the cold world, he must submit — but he forgave them. Then the sobs came thick and fast.

Just at this point he met his soul's sworn comrade, Joe Harper — hard-eyed, and with evidently a great and dismal purpose in his heart. Plainly here were 'two souls with but a single thought'. Tom, wiping his eyes with his sleeve, began to blubber out something about a resolution to escape from hard usage and lack of sympathy at home by roaming abroad into the great world, never to return; and ended by hoping that Joe would not forget him.

But it transpired that this was a request which Joe had just been going to make of Tom, and had come to hunt him up for that purpose. His mother had whipped him for drinking some cream which he had never tasted and knew nothing about; it was plain that she was tired of him and wished him to go; if she felt that way, there was nothing for him to do

but to succumb; he hoped she would be happy, and never regret having
driven her poor boy out into the unfeeling world to suffer and die.

As the two boys walked sorrowing along, they made a new compact to
stand by each other and be brothers, and never separate till death
relieved them of their troubles. Then they began to lay their plans. Joe
was for being a hermit, and living on crusts in a remote cave, and dying,
sometime, of cold, and want, and grief; but, after listening to Tom, he
conceded that there were some conspicuous advantages about a life of
crime, and so he consented to be a pirate.

Three miles below St Petersburg, at a point where the Mississippi river
was a trifle over a mile wide, there was a long, narrow, wooded island,
with a shallow bar at the head of it, and this offered well as a rendezvous.
It was not inhabited; it lay far over towards the farther shore, abreast a
dense and almost wholly unpeopled forest. So Jackson's Island was
chosen. Who were to be the subjects of their piracies was a matter that
did not occur to them. Then they hunted up Huckleberry Finn, and he
joined them promptly, for all careers were one to him; he was
indifferent. They presently separated, to meet at a lonely spot on the
river bank two miles above the village, at the favourite hour, which was
midnight. There was a small log raft there which they meant to capture.
Each would bring hooks and lines, and such provisions as he could steal
in-the most dark and mysterious way — as became outlaws; and before
the afternoon was done, they had all managed to enjoy the sweet glory
of spreading the fact that pretty soon the town would 'hear something'.
All who got this vague hint were cautioned to 'be mum and wait'.

About midnight Tom arrived with a boiled ham and a few trifles, and
stopped in a dense undergrowth on a small bluff overlooking the
meeting-place. It was starlight, and very still. The mighty river lay like
an ocean at rest. Tom listened a moment, but no sound disturbed the
quiet. Then he gave a low, distinct whistle. It was answered from under
the bluff. Tom whistled twice more; these signals were answered in the
same way. Then a guarded voice said:

'Who goes there?'

'Tom Sawyer, the Black Avenger of the Spanish Main. Name your
names.'

'Huck Finn the Red-handed, and Joe Harper the Terror of the Seas.' Tom had furnished these titles from his favourite literature.

''Tis well. Give the countersign.'

Two hoarse whispers delivered the same awful word simultaneously to the brooding night: 'BLOOD!'

Then Tom tumbled his ham over the bluff and let himself down after it, tearing both skin and clothes to some extent in the effort. There was an easy, comfortable path along the shore under the bluff, but it lacked the advantages of difficulty and danger so valued by a pirate.

The Terror of the Seas had brought a side of bacon, and had about worn himself out with getting it there. Finn the Red-handed had stolen a skillet, and a quantity of half-cured leaf-tobacco, and had also brought a few corn-cobs to make pipes with. But none of the pirates smoked or 'chewed' but himself. The Black Avenger of the Spanish Main said it would never do to start without some fire. That was a wise thought; matches were hardly known there in that day. They saw a fire smouldering upon a great raft a hundred yards above, and they went stealthily thither and helped themselves to a chunk. They made an imposing adventure of it, saying 'hist' every now and then and suddenly halting with finger on lip; moving with hands on imaginary dagger hilts; and giving orders in dismal whispers that if 'the foe' stirred to 'let him have it to the hilt', because 'dead men tell no tales'. They knew well enough that the raftmen were all down at the village laying in stores or having a spree, but still that was no excuse for their conducting this thing in an unpiratical way.

from

THE CORAL ISLAND

by R.M. Ballantyne

There was a good deal of jesting at the success of their scheme, as the crew ascended the rocks and addressed the man who had captured me by the title of captain. They were a ferocious set of men, with shaggy beards and scowling brows. All of them were armed with cutlasses and pistols, and their costumes were, with trifling variations, similar to that of the captain. As I looked from one to the other, and observed the low, scowling brows that never unbent, even when the men laughed, and the mean, rascally expression that sat on each face, I felt that my life hung by a hair.

'But where are the other cubs?' cried one of the men, with an oath that made me shudder. 'I'll swear to it there were three, at least, if not more.'

'You hear what he says, whelp: where are the other dogs?'. said the captain.

'If you mean my companions,' said I in a low voice, 'I won't tell you.'

A loud laugh burst from the crew at this answer.

The pirate captain looked at me in surprise. Then drawing a pistol from his belt, he cocked it and said, 'Now, youngster, listen to me. I've no time to waste here. If you don't tell me all you know, I'll blow your brains out! Where are your comrades?'

For an instant I hesitated, not knowing what to do in this extremity. Suddenly a thought occurred to me.

'Villain,' said I, shaking my clenched fist in his face, 'to blow my brains out would make short work of me, and soon be over; death by drowning is as sure, and the agony prolonged: yet I tell you to your face, if you were to toss me over yonder cliff into the sea, I would not tell you where my companions are, and I dare you to try me!'

The pirate captain grew white with rage as I spoke.

'Say you so?' cried he, uttering a fierce oath. — 'Here, lads, take him by the legs and heave him in — quick!'

The men, who were utterly silenced with surprise at my audacity, advanced and seized me, and as they carried me towards the cliff I congratulated myself not a little on the success of my scheme; for I knew that once in the water I should be safe, and could rejoin Jack and Peterkin in the cave. But my hopes were suddenly blasted by the captain crying out, 'Hold on, lads, hold on! We'll give him a taste of the thumb-screws before throwing him to the sharks. Away with him into the boat. Look alive! the breeze is freshening.'

The men instantly raised me shoulder high, and hurrying down the rocks, tossed me into the bottom of the boat, where I lay for some time stunned with the violence of my fall.

On recovering sufficiently to raise myself on my elbow, I perceived that we were already outside the coral reef, and close alongside the schooner, which was of small size and clipper built. I had only time to observe this much, when I received a severe kick on the side from one of the men, who ordered me, in a rough voice, to jump aboard. Rising hastily, I clambered up the side. In a few minutes the boat was hoisted on deck, the vessel's head put close to the wind, and the Coral Island dropped slowly astern as we beat up against a head sea.

Immediately after coming aboard, the crew were too busily engaged in working the ship and getting in the boat to attend to me, so I remained leaning against the bulwarks close to the gangway, watching their operations. I was surprised to find that there were no guns or carronades of any kind in the vessel, which had more the appearance of a fast-sailing trader than a pirate. But I was struck with the neatness of everything. The brass work of the binnacle and about the tiller, as well as the copper belaying-pins, were as brightly polished as if they had just come from the foundry. The decks were pure white, and smooth. The masts were clean-scraped and varnished except at the cross-trees and truck, which were painted black. The standing and running rigging was in the most perfect order, and the sails white as snow. In short, everything from the single narrow red stripe on her low, black hull to the trucks on her tapering masts, evinced an amount of care and strict discipline that would have done credit to a ship of the Royal Navy. There was nothing lumbering or unseemly about the vessel, excepting, perhaps, a boat, which lay on the deck with its keel up between the fore and main masts. It seemed disproportionately large for the schooner; but when I saw that the crew amounted to between thirty and forty men, I concluded that this boat was held in reserve in case of any accident compelling the crew to desert the vessel.

As I have before said, the costumes of the men were similar to that of the captain. But in head-gear they differed not only from him but from each other, some wearing the ordinary straw hat of the merchant service, while others wore cloth caps and red worsted night-caps. I observed that all their arms were sent below, the captain only retaining his cutlass and a single pistol in the folds of his shawl. Although the Captain was the tallest and most powerful man in the ship, he did not strikingly excel many of his men in this respect; and the only difference that an ordinary observer would have noticed was a certain degree of open candour, straight-forward daring, in the bold, ferocious expression of his face, which rendered him less repulsive than his low-browed associates, but did not by any means induce the belief that he was a hero. This look was, however, the indication of that spirit which gave him the pre-eminence among the crew of desperadoes who called him captain. He was a lion-like villain, totally devoid of personal fear, and utterly reckless of consequences, and therefore a terror to his men, who individually hated him but unitedly felt it to be to their advantage to have him at their head.

But my thoughts soon reverted to the dear companions whom I had left on shore, and as I turned towards the Coral Island, which was now far away to leeward, I sighed deeply, and the tears rolled slowly down my cheeks as I thought that I might never see them more.

'So you're blubbering, are you, you obstinate whelp?' said the deep voice of the captain, as he came up and gave me a box on the ear that nearly felled me to the deck. 'I don't allow any such weakness aboard o' this ship. So clap a stopper on your eyes, or I'll give you something to cry for.'

I flushed with indignation at this rough and cruel treatment, but felt that giving way to anger would only make matters worse, so I made no reply, but took out my handkerchief and dried my eyes.

'I thought you were made of better stuff,' continued the captain angrily. 'I'd rather have a mad bulldog aboard than a water-eyed puppy. But I'll cure you, lad, or introduce you to the sharks before long. Now go below, and stay there till I call you.'

As I walked forward to obey, my eye fell on a small keg standing by the side of the main-mast, on which the word *gunpowder* was written in pencil. It immediately flashed across me that, as we were beating up against the wind, anything floating in the sea would be driven on the reef encircling the Coral Island. I also recollected — for thought is more rapid than the lightning — my old companions had a pistol. Without a moment's hesitation, therefore, I lifted the keg from the deck and tossed it into the sea! An exclamation of surprise burst from the captain and some of the men who witnessed this act of mine.

Striding up to me, and uttering fearful imprecations, the captain raised his hand to strike me, while he shouted, 'Boy! whelp! what mean you by that?'

'If you lower your hand,' said I in a loud voice, while I felt the blood rush to my temples, 'I'll tell you. Until you do so I'm dumb.'

The captain stepped back and regarded me with a look of amazement.

'Now,' continued I, 'I threw that keg into the sea because the wind and waves will carry it to my friends on the Coral Island, who happen to have a pistol, but no powder. I hope that it will reach them soon; and my only regret is that the keg was not a bigger one. Moreover, pirate, you said just now that you thought I was made of better stuff. I don't know what stuff I am made of — I never thought much about that subject — but I'm quite certain of this, that I am made of such stuff as the like of you shall never tame, though you should do your worst.'

To my surprise the captain, instead of flying into a rage, smiled, and thrusting his hand into the voluminous shawl that encircled his waist, turned on his heel and walked aft, while I went below.

PIRATES ON FUNAFUTI

by E.V. Rieu

Full many a magic island
      lies within the seas of coral,
But only Funafuti wields
      a magic that is moral.
There is no island of the East
      or in the Spanish Main
That boasts a fauna so correct,
      a flora so urbane.

It is a pretty sight to see
      the billows doff their caps
In breaking on the beach,
      though this is natural perhaps.
The very coconuts that grow
      so slender in the glades
Incline politely to the winds,
      though these are only trades.

One sunny day a pirate band
      approached this happy shore,
Fresh from the looting of a ship,
      and looking out for more —
Jack Slaughter, Galapago Jim,
      Sam Stiff and Hairy Hugh,
Cuthbert the Cook and Barmy Bill —
      they *were* an ugly crew.

The first on Funafuti, as it fell,
    was Captain Jack,
Whom Sam in swinging round an oar
    had landed on his back.
And he rose up in the shallows
    with a murderous grimace —
when an unexpected simper
    altogether changed his face.

'Your pardon, Mr Stiff,' he said,
    'for being in the way.
The fault was mine entirely.
    Not another word, I pray.'
The crew were dumb. 'Be good enough
    to join me on the sand.
Come, Mr Galapago Jim.
    Allow me, Cook, a hand.'

The crew obeyed. They would have feared
    an angry lion less
Than this perplexing suavity,
    this painful *politesse*.
But as in turn they disembarked
    and caught the island's spell
Each felt an impulse to behave
    unusually well.

Said Jim, 'I happen to have brought
    a change in my valise.
Do me the honour, sir, I beg,
    of slipping into these.'
'Your kindly thought,' the Skipper said,
    'may well prevent a chill.
Excuse me for a moment.'
    And he went behind a hill.

And so in all propriety
    they dined upon the beach,
Restricting their consumption
    to a single helping each,
And choosing the right cutlery
    with cultivated ease
For caviare, asparagus,
    or macaroni cheese.

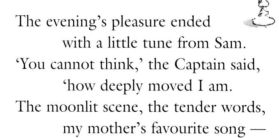

The evening's pleasure ended
    with a little tune from Sam.
'You cannot think,' the Captain said,
    'how deeply moved I am.
The moonlit scene, the tender words,
    my mother's favourite song —
I wonder, O my comrades,
    if a pirate's life is wrong!'

They led him sobbing to his bed,
    their own tears falling fast;
They tucked him in and held his hand
    until the fit had passed;
They smoothed his pillow neatly,
    put his cutlass underneath,
And in a glass beside him
    popped his artificial teeth.

Then one by one they said their prayers
    and folded up their clothes,
Forgetful of the ribald jest,
    the customary oaths;
And with a fairy tale or two
    they talked themselves asleep
To the murmur of the palm-trees
    and the gently stirring deep.

They sailed at dawn.
    And as they left the magic coast behind,
The conduct of the company
    immediately declined.
Their breakfast was a brutal thing;
    at lunch they hardly spoke;
By dinner-time civility
    was treated as a joke.

But still on Funafuti beach
    the ocean rollers break
With a softly silenced thunder,
    lest the little turtles wake;
Clams in their crannies hide their yawns;
    and everything is done
To the perfect satisfaction
    of the overseeing Sun.

from

THE ADVENTURES OF TOM SAWYER

PART II   by Mark Twain

The raft drew beyond the middle of the river; the boys pointed her head right and then lay on their oars. The river was not high, so there was not more than a two or three mile current. Hardly a word was said during the next three-quarters of an hour. Now the raft was passing before the distant town, two or three glimmering lights showed where it lay, peacefully sleeping, beyond the vague was sweep of star-gemmed water, unconscious of the tremendous event that was happening. The Black Avenger stood still with folded arms, 'looking his last' upon the scene of his former joys and his later sufferings, and wishing 'she' could see him, now abroad on the wild sea, facing peril and death with dauntless heart, going to his doom with a grim smile on his lips. It was but a small strain on his imagination to remove Jackson's Island beyond eye-shot of the village, and so he 'looked his last' with a broken and satisfied heart. The other pirates were looking their last, too; and they all looked so long that they came near letting the current drift them out of the range of the island. But they discovered the danger in time, and made shift to avert it. About two o'clock in the morning the raft grounded on the bar two hundred yards above the head of the island, and they waded back and forth until they had landed their freight. Part of the little raft's belongings consisted of an old sail, and this they spread over a nook in the bushes for a tent to shelter their provisions; but they themselves would sleep in the open air in good weather, as became outlaws.

They built a fire against the side of a great log twenty or thirty steps within the sombre depths of the forest, and then cooked some bacon in the frying-pan for supper, and used up half of the corn 'pone' stock they had brought. It seemed glorious sport to be feasting in that wild and free way in the virgin forest of an unexplored and uninhabited island, far from the haunts of men, and they said they would never return to civilization. The climbing fire lit up their faces and threw its ruddy glare upon the pillared tree-trunks of their forest temple, and upon the varnished foliage and festooning vines. When the last crisp slice of bacon was gone, and the last allowance of corn pone devoured, the boys stretched themselves out on the grass, filled with contentment. They could have found a cooler place, but they would not deny themselves such a romantic feature as the roasting camp-fire.

'*Ain't* it jolly?' said Joe.

'It's *nuts*,' said Tom.

'What would the boys say if they could see us?'

'Say? Well, they'd just die to be here — hey, Hucky?'

'I reckon so,' said Huckleberry; 'anyways *I'm* suited. I don't want nothing better'n this. I don't ever get enough to eat gen'ally — and here they can't come and kick at a feller and bullyrag him so.'

'It's just the life for me,' said Tom. 'You don't have to get up, mornings, and you don't have to go to school, and wash, and all that blame foolishness.'

'You see a pirate don't have to do *anything*, Joe, when he's ashore, but a hermit *he* has to be praying considerable, and then he don't have any fun, any way, all by himself that way.'

'Oh yes, that's so,' said Joe, 'but I hadn't thought much about it, you know. I'd a good deal ruther be a pirate now that I've tried it.'

from

MARY READ

told by A.M. Smythe

In the late 17th-century, a young woman, Mary Read, escaped poverty by disguising herself as a man, joining a ship and becoming a pirate.

Once she had taken this desperate step, Mary entered into the life with gusto. She had always been a leader, and a bold one, and now she led a life which knew no standards but courage and resource. She was not ambitious to be captain of a ship. She only wanted to be the first to board the enemy. Most pirates were greedy for gold and wealth, or else afraid either for their necks in this life or their souls in the next. Mary knew neither greed nor fear. She enjoyed this life and did not worry about the next.

The ship cruised about the warm West Indian seas for many months. The crew were experienced sailors and fighters, and knew which ships to challenge and which to leave alone. So all went well. They took several valuable cargoes of naval stores, canvas, pitch, timber, grease, rope, clothes, and ammunition, all being sent from Spain to refit Spanish men-of-war round the coasts of her West Indian empire; or cargoes of gold beating home to Spain from Panama; or fine muslins and silk materials which they could sell again to the colonists in Jamaica and other islands at high prices; or drugs and medicines, all of enormous value; or holds full of barrels of wine which were broached to warm the pirates' hearts and illumine many a wild night.

As on most pirate ships, discipline was severe, and so the crew lived at peace with each other, though at war with the whole world. One among the crew became particularly friendly with Mary. After a time Mary's suspicions were aroused, and she discovered that he, too, was a woman in disguise. Her name was Anne Bonny. She was a gay, lawless Irishwoman after Mary's own heart. They both swore to keep each other's secret, and kept the promise faithfully. They became comrades in arms, and the crew vowed there were no sailors on the seas more resolute, more ready to board the enemy or to attempt any hazard. So they lived for many months in their dark, evil-smelling, crowded ship, hot and verminous below, but above decks neat and trim, and cheered by the balmy air of the West Indies.

But though she might forget it, Mary was a woman still, and a beautiful one. One day the pirates took a prize, and among the captives was a young man who was gently born and had no desire to be a pirate. To Mary, watching him as he toiled among his savage companions at unaccustomed work, or sat at the rough drunken meals, he brought back an air from another, forgotten world. He was brave and quick, and held his own with the pirates, but he was different from them, and Mary loved him.

For the second time in her wild life she was conquered, and again by love. She made friends with the young man, and when she found that he was drawn to her, she told him she was a woman. They were married as best they could be, in secret and without a priest, and began one of the strangest married lives ever known, among the pirates.

Mary loved him, as she did everything, with her whole heart. To her horror one day he told her that he had quarrelled with the most savage member of the crew, called the Bull, and in accordance with the pirate rules had to fight a duel with him on shore that evening. Mary was desperate. She and her husband took out the ship's dinghy and pulled about the harbour, one of their few devices to be alone together during the day.

'He will kill you, I know he will!' she declared.

'Nonsense! I'm as good a swordsman, and he'll be drunk.'

'You talk like a fine gentleman,' she broke in. 'As good a swordsman! Of course you are, but the Bull won't fight fair. I tell you, he has fought a dozen of these duels, and though he is no swordsman he has always been the one to come back alive. You don't know him. He's probably even now preparing the ground and digging some trap for you.'

Her husband was aghast.

'What shall I do? I can't draw back.'

'No!' flashed Mary. 'They'd always say you were a coward, and some night you'd get a knife in your back.'

'Well, I shall fight him, and I'll keep a sharp look-out. He deserves

killing, and I shall kill him.'

But Mary was not to be cheered. She asked him the time of the duel, and he said seven o'clock; then they pulled back to the ship. Mary went to look for the Bull. She found him in a crowd, lazily boasting of how he was going to carve up the young man that evening. She listened for a time, her heart beating heavily, her hands cold.

'That'll be the end of him, the young dog!' said the Bull. 'And a good riddance, too; he's no pirate.'

They all laughed, and then Mary said in her clear voice:

'Nor is the Bull a true man! He only fights with boys and prisoners.'

A gasp ran round the group. Such a remark meant only one thing. The Bull sat up slowly on the deck, his face growing dark. He looked at Mary, and she at him.

'You think yourself a pretty good fighter, don't you?' said the Bull. 'And you're neither boy nor prisoner, though you're an undersized little rat. Well, I'll fight you at any time and place you like to choose, and then we'll be rid of another pest.'

Everyone was watching with bated breath.

'All right,' Mary replied coolly. 'Five o'clock this evening. I've been wanting to clean the ship up for a long time. Five o'clock behind the last bungalow.' She sauntered away.

She went to her bunk and spent the time cleaning her pistols. She refused to listen to any persuasion from her husband. At half-past four she rowed herself ashore, and approached the last bungalow of the village from a safe and unexpected angle. The Bull was there, and she hailed him.

'Come over here,' he growled.

'No, thanks. I'm choosing time and place, and it's healthier over here.' She was certain that he had been making a trap. He shambled forward, his tasselled cap hanging over his swollen, purple face. As he came, she saw his hand move and she ducked as a ball whistled over her head. In rage he fired again, and she knew his pistol was useless unless he could reload. She meant to shoot him down as he was dragging out his curved sword, but on a swift instinct for a fight she seized her sword and sprang to her feet. They closed, and Mary rejoiced in the knowledge that she was the better swordsman. The Bull puffed and cursed, but his wild blows could not break Mary's guard. In a few moments her sword slipped under his, and ran the Bull through. As he staggered she leapt back, and, snatching her pistol, gave him both barrels through the head. Leaving the body, she went back to her boat and rowed calmly to the ship and rejoined her husband. He swore that there was indeed no wife in the world like her.

from

TREASURE ISLAND

by Robert Louis Stevenson

The parrot sat, preening her plumage, on Long John's shoulder. He himself, I thought, looked somewhat paler and more stern than I was used to. He still wore the fine broadcloth suit in which he had fulfilled his mission, but it was bitterly the worst for wear, daubed with clay and torn with the sharp briers of the wood.

'So,' said he, 'here's Jim Hawkins, shiver my timbers! dropped in, like, eh? Well, come, I take that friendly.'

And thereupon he sat down upon the brandy cask, and began to fill a pipe.

'Give me a loan of the link, Dick,' said he; and then, when he had a good light, 'that'll do, lad,' he added; 'stick the glim in the wood heap,' and you, gentlemen, bring yourselves to! — and needn't stand up for Mr Hawkins; *he'll* excuse you, you may lay to that. And so, Jim' — stopping the tobacco — 'here you were, and quite a pleasant surprise for poor old John, I see you were smart when first I set my eyes on you; but this here gets away from me clean, it do.'

To all this, as may be well supposed, I made no answer. They had set me with my back against the wall; and I stood there, looking Silver in the face, pluckily enough, I hope, to all outward appearance, but with black despair in my heart.

Silver took a whiff or two of his pipe with great composure, and then ran on again.

'Now, you see, Jim, so be as you *are* here,' says he, 'I'll give you a piece of my mind, I've always liked you, I have, for a lad of spirit, and the picter of my own self when I was young and handsome. I always wanted you to jine and take your share, and die a gentleman, and now, my cock, you've got to. Cap'n Smollett's a fine seaman, as I'll own up to any day, but stiff on discipline. "Dooty is dooty," says he, and right he is. Just you keep clear of the cap'n. The doctor himself is gone dead again — "ungrateful scamp" was what he said; and the short and the long of the whole story is about here: you can't go back to your own lot, for they won't have you; and without you start a third ship's company all by yourself, which might be lonely, you'll have to jine up with Cap'n Silver.'

So far so good. My friends, then, were still alive, and though I partly believed the truth of Silver's statement, that the cabin party were incensed at me for my desertion, I was more relieved than distressed by what I heard.

'I don't say nothing as to your being in our hands,' continued Silver, 'though there you are, and you may lay to it, I'm all for argyment; I never seen good come out o' threatening. If you like the service, well, you'll jine; and if you don't, Jim, why, you're free to answer no — free and welcome, shipmate; and if fairer can be said by mortal seaman, shiver my sides!'

'Am I to answer then?' I asked, with a very tremulous voice. Through all this sneering talk, I was made to feel the threat of death that overhung me, and my cheeks burned and my heart beat painfully in my breast.

'Lad,' said Silver, 'no-one's a-pressing of you. Take your bearings, None of us won't hurry you, mate; time goes so pleasant in your company, you see.'

'Well,' says I, growing a bit bolder, 'if I'm to choose, I declare I have a right to know what's what, and why you're here, and where my friends are.'

'Wots wot?' repeated one of the buccaneers, in a deep growl. 'Ah, he'd be a lucky one as knowed that!'

'You'll, perhaps, batten down your hatches till you're spoke to, my friend, ' cried Silver truculently to this speaker. And then, in his first gracious tones, he replied to me: 'Yesterday morning, Mr Hawkins,' said he, 'in the dogwatch, down came Doctor Livesey with a flag of truce.

Says he, "Cap'n Silver, you're sold out. Ship's gone." Well, maybe we'd been taking a glass, and a song to help it round. I won't say no. Leastways, none of us had looked out. We looked out, and, by thunder! the old ship was gone. I never seen a pack of fools look fishier; and you may lay to that, if I tells you that looked the fishiest. "Well," says the doctor, "let's bargain." We bargained, him and I, and here were are: stores, brandy, block-house, the firewood you was thoughtful enough to cut, and, in a manner of speaking, the whole blessed boat, from cross-trees to kelson. As for them, they've tramped; I don't know where they are.'

He drew again quietly at his pipe.

'And lest you should take it into that head of your,' he went on , 'that you was included in the treaty, here's the last word that was said: "How many are you," says I, "to leave?" "Four," says he — "four, and one of us wounded. As for that boy, I don't know where he is, confound him," says he, "nor I don't much care. We're about sick of him." These were his words.'

'Is that all?' I asked.

'Well, it's all that you're to hear, my son,' returned Silver.

'And now I am to choose?'

'And now you are to choose, and you may lay to that,' said Silver.

'Well,' said I, 'I am not such a fool but I know pretty well what I have to look for. Let the worst come to the worst, it's little I care. I've seen too many die since I fell in with you,' I said, and by this time I was quite excited; 'and the first is this: here you are, in a bad way: ship lost, treasure lost, men lost; your whole business go to wreck; and if you want to know who did it — it was I! I was in the apple barrel the night we sighted land, and I heard you, John, and you, Dick Johnson, and Hands, who is now at the bottom of the sea, and told every word you said before the hour was out. And as for the schooner, it was I who cut her cable, and it was I that killed the men you had aboard of her, and it was I who brought her where you'll never see her more, not one of you. The laugh's on my side; I've had the top of this business from the first; I no more fear you than I fear a fly. Kill me, if you please, or spare me. But one thing I'll say, and no more; if you spare me, bygones are bygones, and when you fellows are in court for piracy, I'll save you all I can. It is for you to choose. Kill another and do yourselves no good, or spare me and keep a witness to save you from the gallows.'

I stopped, for, I tell you, I was out of breath, and, to my wonder, not a man of them moved, but all sat staring at me like as many sheep. And while they were still staring, I broke out again:

'And now, Mr Silver,' I said, 'I believe you're the best man here, and if things go to the worst, I'll take it kind of you to let the doctor know the way I took it.'

'I'll bear it in mind,' said Silver, with an accent so curious that I could not, for the life of me, decide whether he were laughing at my request, or had been favourably affected by my courage.

'I'll put one to that,' cried the old mahogany-faced seaman — Morgan by name — whom I had seen in Long John's public-house upon the quays of Bristol. 'It was him that knowed Black Dog.'

'Well and see here,' Added the sea-cook. 'I'll put another again, by thunder! for it was this same boy that faked the chart from Billy Bones.

First and last, we've split upon Jim Hawkins!'

'Then here goes!' said Morgan, with an oath.

And he sprang up, drawing his knife as if he had been twenty.

'Avast there!' cried Silver. 'Who are you, Tom Morgan? Maybe you thought you was cap'n here, perhaps. By the powers, but I'll teach you better! Cross me, and you'll go where many a good man's gone before you, first and last, these thirty year back — some of them to the yard-arm, shiver my timbers! and some by the board, and all to feed the fishes. There's never a man looked me between the eyes and seen a good day a'terwards, Tom Morgan, you may lay to that.'

Morgan paused; but a hoarse murmur rose from the others.

'Tom's right,' said one.

'I stood hazing long enough from one,' added another. 'I'll be hanged if I'll be hazed by you, John Silver.'

'Did any of you gentlemen want to have it out with *me*?' roared Silver, bending far forward from his position on the keg, with his pipe still glowing in his right hand. 'Put a name on what you're at; you aint dumb, I reckon. Him that wants shall get it. Have I lived this many years, and a son of a rum puncheon cock his hat athwart my hawse at the latter end of it? You know the way; you're all gentlemen o'fortune, by your account. Well, I'm ready. Take a cutlass, him that dares, and I'll see the colour of his inside, crutch and all, before that pipe's empty.'

Not a man stirred; not a man answered.

'That's your sort, is it?' he added, returning his pipe to his mouth. 'Well, you're a gay lot to look at, anyway. Not much worth to fight, you aint. P'r'aps you can understand King George's English. I'm cap'n here by 'lection. I'm cap'n here because I'm the best man by a long sea-mile. You won't fight, as gentlemen o'fortune should; then, by thunder, you'll obey, and you may lay to it! I like that boy, now, I never seen a better boy than that. He's more a man than any pair of rats of you in this here house, and what I say is this: let me see him that'll lay a hand on him — that's what I say, and you may lay to it.'

There was a long pause after this. I stood straight up against the wall, my heart still going like a sledge-hammer, but with a ray of hope now shining in my bosom.

from

THE ADVENTURES OF TOM SAWYER

PART III   by Mark Twain

Presently Huck said:

'What do pirates have to do?'

Tom said:

'Oh, they just have a bully time — take ships, and burn them, and get the money and bury it in awful places in their island where there's ghosts and things to watch it, and kill everybody in the ships — make 'em walk a plank.'

'And they carry the women to the island,' said Joe; 'they don't kill the women.'

'No,' assented Tom, 'they don't kill the women — they're too noble. And the women's always beautiful too.'

'And don't they wear the bulliest clothes! Oh, no! All gold and silver and di'monds,' said Joe with enthusiasm.

'Who?' said Huck.

'Why, the pirates.'

Huck scanned his own clothing forlornly.

'I reckon I ain't dressed fitten for a pirate,' said he, with a regretful pathos in his voice; 'but I ain't got none but these.'

But the other boys told him the fine clothes would come fast enough after they should have begun their adventures. They made him understand that his poor rags would do to begin with, though it was customary for wealthy pirates to start with a proper wardrobe.

Gradually their talk died out and drowsiness began to steal upon the eyelids of the little waifs. The pipe dropped from the fingers of the Red-handed, and he slept the sleep of the conscience-free and the weary. The

Terror of the Seas and the Black Avenger of the Spanish Main had more difficulty in getting to sleep. They said their prayers inwardly, and lying down, since there was nobody there with authority to make them kneel and recite out loud; in truth they had a mind not to say them at all, but they were afraid to proceed to such lengths as all that, lest they might call down a sudden and special thunder-bolt from heaven. Then at once they reached and hovered upon the imminent verge of sleep — but an intruder came now that would not 'down'. It was conscience. They began to feel a vague fear that they had been doing wrong to run away; and next they thought of the stolen meat, and then the real torture came. They tried to argue it away by reminding conscience that they had purloined sweetmeats and apples scores of times; but conscience was not to be appeased by such thin plausibilities. It seemed to them, in the end, that there was no getting around the stubborn fact that taking sweetmeats was only 'hooking' while taking bacon and ham and such valuables was plain, simple stealing — and there was a command against that in the Bible. So they inwardly resolved that so long as they remained in the business, their piracies should not again be sullied with the crime of stealing. Then conscience granted a truce, and these curiously inconsistent pirates fell peacefully to sleep.

SAILORS' LORE

*SUPERSTITIONS
AND LEGENDS
OF THE SEA*

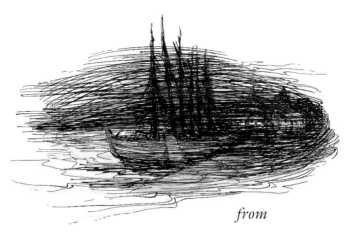

from

THE MERMAID OF EMMELOORD

PART I   by Jan de Hartog

One night, almost a year after Jan had got lost, a night when there was no moon and no breeze and fog enclosed the Island of Schockland, Mensje looked up in the lamplight, amazed, for she heard distinctly the splash and the rattle of an anchor dropping in the bay. That was very strange, for there was no wind and no visibility; the ships in the harbour were lying dead, the ropes silent against the masts and everybody in the village was asleep in the comfortable certainty that no ship could reach the island that night.

She got up, put her shawl around her shoulders, went out and climbed the dike. She had been used to walking along it to the jetty, for that was where all the boats moored, but the night was so thick with fog that she couldn't see one step in front of her, and so she stood still, listening.

She heard distinctly the creaking of oars approaching in the fog, the murmur of water against the bow of a boat, she even heard the oarsmen sighing and the soft clanking of the rubber chain, but she saw nothing. The sounds seemed to come straight at her, and for the first time since Jan had left she became conscious of being alone.

Then there was the scraping of an iron keel on the basalt of the dike, the rumbling of oars being pulled in, the splashing of people getting out and wading through the shallow water; then suddenly, there came a faint light climbing towards her, with the scraping of hob-nailed boots on the rocks.

The light came nearer and nearer, until she saw that it was a very old-fashioned lantern. Then it stood still, and the steps fell silent. She saw only that lantern, and nothing else; but she knew there must be men around it, hidden in the fog, and she asked her question without seeing whom she was addressing.

'Have you seen the *Rising Hope*, the flagship of the East India Company?' she asked, and for the first time she realized how often she had asked it before. The lantern shone motionlessly in the fog, and she was about to turn away when a voice said: 'We have.'

She took a long time asking her second question, for she had suddenly become afraid. This was the answer she had been waiting for, for almost a year; but now that she finally heard it a cold fear started creeping up her legs. 'Have you heard any news about Jan Viool, a sailor?' she asked. 'He may have changed ships abroad.'

Again the lantern shone motionlessly in the fog for minutes on end, before the voice answered: 'We have.'

The fear had crept up so high now, that it nearly numbed her lips. 'Do you know where he is?' she whispered.

Again the voice answered: 'We do.'

Then she asked her last question, and even before she had spoken she realized that it was going to decide her life. Asking that question was the bravest thing she had ever done; but as she decided that she would help Jan even if it would cost everything she had, she looked at the motionless lantern bravely and said: 'Could you take me to him?'

The silence that met her question lasted so long that she repeated it. Then the voice said: 'We can. But it will cost you a lot.'

'It doesn't matter,' she said. 'You can have anything I possess; tell me your price.'

The voice answered: 'It will cost you your soul.'

AN UNEVENTFUL VOYAGE
by Hilaire Belloc

At sea the days go slipping past.
Monotonous from first to last —
A trip like any other one
In vessels going south. The sun
Grew higher and more fiery.

We lay and drank, and swore, and played
At Trick-my-neighbour in the shade;
and you may guess how every sight,
However trivial or slight,
Was noted in my diary.
I have it here — the usual things —
A serpent (not the sort with wings)
Came rising from the sea:
In length (as far as we could guess)
A quarter of a mile or less.
The weather was extremely clear
The creature dangerously near
And plain as it would be.
It had a bifurcated tail,
And in its mouth it held a whale.

Just north, I find, of Cape de Verd
We caught a very curious bird
    With horns upon its head;
And — not, as one might well suppose,
Web-footed or with jointed toes —
    But having hoofs instead.
As no one present seemed to know
Its use or name, I let it go.

On June the 7th after dark
A young and very hungry shark
    Came climbing up the side.
It ate the Chaplain and the Mate —
But why these incidents relate?
    The public must decide,
That nothing in the voyage out
Was worth their bothering about.
    Until we saw the coast, which looks
Exactly as it does in books.

How the Whale got his Throat

by Rudyard Kipling

In the sea, once upon a time, O my Best Beloved, there was a Whale, and he ate fishes. He ate the starfish and the garfish, and the crab and the dab, and the plaice and the dace, and the skate and his mate, and the mackereel and the pickereel, and the really truly twirly-whirly eel. All the fishes he could find in all the sea he ate with his mouth — so! Till at last there was only one small fish left in all the sea, and he was a small 'Stute Fish, and he swam a little behind the Whale's right ear, so as to be out of harm's way. Then the Whale stood up on his tail and said, 'I'm hungry.' And the small 'Stute Fish said in a small 'stute voice, 'Noble and generous Cetacean, have you ever tasted Man?'

'No,' said the Whale. 'What is it like?'

'Nice,' said the small 'Stute Fish. 'Nice but nubbly.'

'Then fetch me some,' said the Whale, and he made the sea froth up with his tail.

'One at a time is enough,' said the 'Stute Fish. 'If you swim to latitude Fifty North, longitude Forty West (that is Magic), you will find, sitting *on* a raft, *in* the middle of the sea, with nothing on but a pair of blue canvas breeches, a pair of suspenders (you must *not* forget the suspenders, Best Beloved), *and* a jack-knife, one ship-wrecked Mariner, who, it is only fair to tell you, is a man of infinite-resource-and-sagacity.'

So the Whale swam and swam to latitude Fifty North, longitude Forty West, as fast as he could swim, and *on* a raft, *in* the middle of the sea, with, nothing to wear except a pair of blue canvas breeches, a pair of suspenders (you must particularly remember the suspenders, Best Beloved), *and* a jack-knife, he found one single, solitary shipwrecked Mariner, trailing his toes in the water. (He had his Mummy's leave to paddle, or else he would never have done it, because he was a man of infinite-resource-and-sagacity.)

Then the Whale opened his mouth back and back and back till it nearly touched his tail, and he swallowed the shipwrecked Mariner, and the raft he was sitting on, and his blue canvas breeches, and the suspenders (which you *must* not forget), *and* the jack-knife. He swallowed them all down into his warm, dark, inside cupboards, and then he smacked his lips — so, and turned round three times on his tail.

But as soon as the Mariner, who was a man of infinite-resource-and-sagacity, found himself truly inside the Whale's warm, dark, inside cupboards, he stumped and he jumped and he thumped and he bumped, and he pranced and he danced, and he banged and he clanged, and he hit and he bit, and he leaped and he creeped, and he prowled and he howled, and he hopped and he dropped, and he cried and he sighed, and he crawled and he bawled, and he stepped and he lepped, and he danced hornpipes where he shouldn't, and the Whale felt most unhappy indeed. (*Have* you forgotten the suspenders?)

So he said to the 'Stute Fish, 'This man is very nubbly, and besides he is making me hiccough. What shall I do?'

'Tell him, to come out,' said the 'Stute Fish.

So the Whale called down his own throat to the shipwrecked Mariner, 'Come out and behave yourself. I've got the hiccoughs.'

'Nay, nay!' said the Mariner. 'Not so, but far otherwise. Take me to my natal-shore and the white-cliffs-of-Albion, and I'll think about it.' And he began to dance more than ever.

'You had better take him home,' said the 'Stute Fish to the Whale. 'I ought to have warned you that he is a man of infinite-resource-and-sagacity.'

So the Whale swam and swam and swam, with both flippers and his tail, as hard as he could for the hiccoughs; and at last he saw the Mariner's natal-shore and the white-cliffs-of-Albion, and he rushed half-way up the beach, and opened his mouth wide and wide and wide, and said, 'Change here for Winchester, Ashuelot, Nashua, Keene, and stations on the *Fitch*burg Road'; and just as he said 'Fitch' the Mariner walked out of his mouth. But while the Whale had been swimming, the Mariner, who was indeed a person of infinite-resource-and-sagacity, had taken his jack-knife and cut up the raft into a little square grating all running criss-cross, and he had tied it firm with his suspenders (*now* you know why you were not to forget the suspenders!), and he dragged that grating good and tight into the Whale's throat, and there it stuck! Then he recited the following *Sloka*, which, as you have not heard it, I will now proceed to relate:

> By means of a grating
> I have stopped your ating.

For the Mariner he was also an Hi-ber-ni-an. And he stepped out on the shingle, and went home to his Mother, who had given him leave to trail his toes in the water; and he married and lived happily ever afterward. So did the Whale. But from that day on, the grating in his throat, which he could neither cough up or swallow down, prevented him eating anything except very, very small fish; and that is the reason why whales nowadays never eat men or boys or little girls.

The small 'Stute Fish went and hid himself in the mud under the Doorsills of the Equator. He was afraid that the Whale might be angry with him.

The Sailor took the jack-knife home. He was wearing the blue canvas breeches when he walked out on the shingle. The suspenders were left behind, you see, to tie the grating with; and that is the end of *that* tale.

When the cabin port holes are dark and green
Because of the seas outside;
When the ship goes *wop* (with a wiggle between)
And the steward falls into the soup tureen,
And the trunks begin to slide;
When Nursey lies on the floor in a heap,
And Mummy tells you to let her sleep,
And you aren't waked or washed or dressed,
Why, then you will know (if you haven't guessed)
You're 'Fifty North and Forty West!'

from

THE MERMAID OF EMMELOORD

PART II   by Jan de Hartog

When she woke up again the lantern shone no more. The cabin was light: the curious blue-green light she knew so well from her dream. The first thing she saw gave her a shiver of terror: her hair seemed to be standing on end, it rose to the ceiling and moved softly, waving about. She was so cold that it felt as if her body wasn't there any longer; when she swung the blanket aside it was much lighter than it had been the night before.

But she didn't notice this, for when she swung the blanket aside she saw a sight that nearly made her heart stop: the lower part of her body had changed into a glistening fishtail.

While she lay staring, aghast, at her scales and the forked fin that had once been her feet, a swift shadow passed above her. When she looked up she saw it was a little fish, that had swum in through the open porthole and now floated in the middle of the cabin. The little fish stared at her curiously out of the side of its head with one gold eye, then it turned, swam around the lantern, dived and nibbled at her clothes. When she slowly stretched out her hand towards it, it flashed away, a streak of silver, and shot out of the porthole into the green light. She rose on her elbows and was amazed how light she was; then she looked out of the porthole and saw where she was.

The ship was lying in the deserted market-place of a village of ruins. On the other side of the market-place was a roofless church of red bricks, its tower broken; and the tower was covered with the curious creeper that she had never been able to recognise until this moment. It was seaweed.

She got out of the bunk, but never touched the floor, for she floated. Her tail was very strong; when she made a movement of walking she shot ahead and bumped her head against the wall, but her cry of pain was soundless. She understood that she was now in a world of gentle movements and silence.

She tried to open the door but found it was still locked; then she swung around and a quiver of her tail sent her soaring towards the porthole. She stretched her arms through it and tried to make her body follow, but the porthole was too narrow. Then she gave one strong sweep with her tail, and with a tearing pain she shot out into the green light, rose high up in the sky, turned, circled over the roofs of the ruins and descended gently at the bottom of the broken tower, the very spot where Jan had stood.

While she hovered there sadly, looking around for her lost lover, an old man crossed the market-place with slow long steps, rising into the air at each step as if he danced. She stirred her tail and flashed towards him so fast that she had to rise over his head and circle around before she cautiously descended beside him. He was a very old man with one eye and old-fashioned clothes; on the top of his bald head was a brand-mark of a skull and cross-bones, and she understood that he was a pirate. She had a moment of fear, but the thought that she could flash out of his reach with one sweep of her tail gave her a feeling of security. The old man didn't look a bit amazed on seeing her; his one eye gazed at her sadly, as if the sight of her filled him with pity.

She wondered how to communicate with him in this soundless world, but he took her head between his hands, pressed his cold lips against her ear and she heard a whisper. 'Jan Viool has just left.' Then the old man pointed at the green dusk behind the town, and moved his lips as if to say good-bye. She hesitated, for the dusk seemed to be filled with fear: slowly rising in blue circles, waving with the limp dead trees of seaweed, floating with the fleeting shadows of unseen fish. But she thought of Jan and his despair, swung her tail and shot away into the terror of that unknown world, her long hair streaming behind her, spurred by the one hope left to her: that one day, one night, she would find him.

from

THE MYSTERY OF THE MARY CELESTE

told by Maurice Saxby

It was midwinter, and the *Dei Gratia*, sailing from New York to Gibraltar, was heaving its way through the grey-green Atlantic Ocean. Captain Moorehouse was on watch when he saw, to the windward, a ship being tossed about, reeling drunkenly through the waves as though there was no one at the helm. Only two of its sails were set, the rest hung in tatters or were furled. Shouting to the first mate, a Mr Devereau, to take the helm, Captain Moorehouse brought the *Dei Gratia* close by the helpless ship.

'Brig ahoy! Brig ahoy!' he shouted through the megaphone, all the time scanning the deck for signs of life. Not a soul was to be seen. The ship seemed deserted. A torn and tattered Stars and Stripes flapped in the wind, and as the *Dei Gratia* closed in, Captain Moorehouse could read the name on the stern — *Mary Celeste*.

Turning to his first mate, Captain Moorehouse yelled through the wind, 'She seems abandoned. Best we go aboard, Mr Devereau.' And they did. Devereau, John Wright the second mate, and one of the hands lowered the long boat and pulled alongside the *Mary Celeste*. There was no reply when they hailed the ship again — and the deck was utterly empty of life. It was no easy job clambering aboard a lurching ship in a tossing sea. But Devereau and Wright heaved themselves on board, knowing now that something uncanny had come their way. Cautiously they began to move about the deserted ship, and as they stepped through the water that was lapping across the sill of the galley, shivers began to run up and down their spines. Had the dreaded Yellow Fever broken out among the crew? What would they find if they ventured below? Had the ship been captured by some terrible assailant who lurked silently somewhere on board? Dreaded possibilities raced through the minds of the two men as they carefully began to explore the mystery ship.

Not one clue did they find. The cabins were as empty as the

deckhouse, although everything was in shipshape order. In the saloon, the table was set for dinner, and in the captain's cabin a melodeon with sheet music open on the stand was open as though it had just been played. On a small deck by the same cabin there was a sewing machine that must have belonged to the captain's wife, with some pieces of sewing and a child's toy nearby. In the crew's quarters ungathered washing was hanging on lines. It was as though an invisible hand had swept every living creature on board into oblivion.

The seamen from *Dei Gratia* felt tremors of fear surging through their bodies as they went below into the hold which was loaded with a cargo of alcohol and contained sufficient stores to last at least six months. There was plenty of fresh water, and the seawater which was washing around below could have been pumped out in a couple of hours. So what could have happened?

Retracing their steps, Devereau and Wright searched the *Mary Celeste* again, poking into every nook and cranny. Only two things stood out in their minds. One barrel of alcohol had been emptied. But that was not so surprising, and there was no sign of a drunken spree. More significantly, there was an upturned hatch on the deck — something no experienced captain or seaman would allow. That, too, was a bad omen in the lore of the sea. But what — what could possibly have caused the disappearance of every soul on board a ship in the middle of the Atlantic Ocean in the year of our Lord, 1872? To this day, nobody has solved *that* mystery.

THE KRAKEN

by Alfred, Lord Tennyson

Below the thunders of the upper deep;
Far far beneath in the abysmal sea,
His ancient, dreamless, uninvaded sleep
The Kraken sleepeth: faintest sunlights flee
About his shadowy sides: above him swell
Huge sponges of millennial growth and height;
And far away into the sickly light,
From many a wondrous grot and secret cell
Unnumber'd and enormous polypi
Winnow with giant fins the slumbering green.
There hath he lain for ages and will lie
Battening upon huge seaworms in his sleep,
Until the latter fire shall heat the deep;
Then once by men and angels to be seen,
In roaring he shall rise and on the surface die.

from

THE MERMAID OF EMMELOORD

PART III

by Jan de Hartog

Amid the mussels and the barnacles she found after searching for a long time, a huge rusty iron ring, like a door knocker, and using all her strength she swung it to and fro until at last it knocked. There was a sound of heavy bolts, a creaking of huge hinges, and the crack got wider until a flat beam of golden light shone into the green darkness of the weeds like sunlight falling into a wood.

In that light she saw the face of a very old man with a white beard appear, and his blue innocent eyes gazed at her in amazement. He must be one of the apostles, and somehow she knew instantly that he was Peter. When she spoke she discovered that she had suddenly got her voice back; it sounded faint and distant, but it was unmistakably hers.

'Could you tell me,' she asked, 'where I can find Jan Viool, a sailor?'

'Who are you?' the old man asked gently.

'I am his girl,' she said.

Old Peter looked at her intently, and then his face changed; as if only at that moment he realised that she was a mermaid.

'You are just a few days too late,' he said. 'He went back to the Island of Schokland the day before yesterday, alive again.'

She felt a terrible sadness and at the same time a great joy overcame her, and when she repeated: 'Alive!' she felt something warm go down her cheeks, the first warmth she had felt since she had woken up in that cabin of stone, long ago.

'Yes,' said Peter, while shutting the door. 'He has been lucky: some fool ashore has given up his soul for him.'

121

She didn't know what to say any more. She saw, through her tears, the sunlight shrink to a vanishing crack; then it was dark again around her, and she sank slowly down along the chain until she was back in the desert, where the huge rusty blade of the anchor lay waiting to be lifted from the sand at Judgement Day.

She sat down on the anchor, and wept. She was quite alone. The thought of wandering among the drowned for ever without even the hope of ever reaching the man she loved made her very sad, and for a while it seemed to her as if now there was nothing left to live for. But then she thought of his despair when he would arrive in the Island of Schokland and find her gone, and it was that thought that made her sweep her tail and shoot back into the horror of the black forest, across the nightmarish miles of sunken jungle, across ocean and seas, until at last she reached the dike over which she saw the timid roofs of Emmeloord peeping at the horizon.

On the dike stood a lonely man, staring sadly at the sea. She rose from the waves and waved, but he didn't see her. She called his name, but he didn't hear her. She pleaded, shouted, jumped out of the water with a burst of silver spray, lashing the waves with her tail; but he saw and heard nothing. He sighed, and he turned slowly around, and vanished behind the dike to go into the little house, in which she knew he would lie down and dream of a girl, standing at the foot of a broken red tower covered with seaweed, smiling at him through a green glass plate, and forming three small words with her lips which he would, one night, perhaps understand.

Jan Viool became the lighthouse keeper of Schokland and remained a brooder until the end of his life; but the mermaid, who was immortal, realised in the end that all men were brothers, and her love became like a fountain; it shot up towards one sailor, but it rained down on all of them. She remained in the sea around the Island of Schokland until this day, and every time a storm is brewing the fishermen hear a soft girl's voice, singing above the murmur of the waves. When they hear it they furl their sails, lock their cabins and go home to wait in bed with their wives until the gale is over, which they know will come before the dawn.

Glossary of Nautical Terms

aft near or towards the back

astern towards the stern; behind

backstays ropes extending from the mast to the sides of a ship, slanting backwards slightly

barque a small three-masted sailing ship

belaying-pins iron or wood bars with which to secure rigging, sometimes used as weapons

berth either a ship's room or when a ship is moored

binnacle a box containing the ship's compass

boom a pole used to extend the foot of a sail

bow the front part of a boat

brig a two-masted, square-rigged sailing ship

bulwarks the part above the ship's deck, often used during battle

buoy a floating marker

burgee a small flag flown at mast-head for identification and as a wind-vane

clipper a large fast-sailing vessel used in the 19th century

close-hauled sailing as near as possible to the wind

coracle a small primitive boat

cross-trees strong horizontal timbers at the top of the mast to support the rigging

deadeye a block with three holes for tightening a rope

flying jib a small triangular sail

foghorn a horn used as a warning signal in bad weather

forecastle the living quarters of the crew in merchant ships, or the cabin at the front of the boat

furled sails rolled up, not in use

gangway a platform providing access to and from a ship

hold a space below decks used for storage or cargo

hull the body of the boat excluding the masts and rigging

inboard inside the body of the ship

jib a triangular sail at the front of a boat

jibe to alter course by allowing a sail to swing from one side of the boat to the other

jibsheet a line or rope used to adjust the position of the jib in relation to the wind

keel attached to the base of a boat to keep it upright in the water

lee side the sheltered side, away from the direction of the wind

main yard a pole used to extend the mainsail

mainsail the principal sail, attached to the mainmast

mainsheet a rope attached to the lower corner of the mainsail to adjust its position

outrigger a projecting spar for extending sails

port the left-hand side of a boat

porthole a window or opening in a ship's side

prow the front part of a boat

quarter-deck part of the deck usually reserved for officers

ratlines ropes secured horizontally across the shrouds to act as the rungs of a ladder

rowlocks the fittings into which oars are secured

royal mast-head above the main top gallant mast, used in fine weather

royal yard the highest sail on the main mast

rudder part of the boat used for steering

schooner a fast-sailing vessel, originally two-masted but can have up to six masts

sculls light oars used for rowing

ship's waist part of the ship between the quarter-deck and the forecastle; the worst position in times of action

shoals patches of shallow water

shrouds a set of ropes running from the top of the mast to the sides of the boat to support the mast

spar a pole, can refer to a mast or boom

starboard the right-hand side of a boat

stay a rope supporting a mast, running from the mast to a securing point either fore or aft

steerage the cheapest, most cramped, living quarters on a ship

stern the back part of a boat from which to steer

tiller the handle or horizontal bar which is joined to the rudder to steer the boat

topgallant spar below the royal mast, carries the topgallant sails

topsail spar attaches the topsail across the topmast

trestletrees short timbers supporting the topmast and its rigging

truck a cap at the top of a mast

trysail a small sail, often used in storms

watch a sailor's period of duty during a voyage

yard-arm the outermost part of a yard (a spar fastened to a mast). Used for flying signals and also the part from which men sentenced to death by court-martial were hanged

ACKNOWLEDGEMENTS

The Publishers gratefully acknowledge the following for permission to reproduce copyright material in this book:

'Boating' © James Reeves from *Complete Poems for Children* (Heinemann). Reprinted by permission of the James Reeves Estate.

Extract from *The Little Grey Men* © B.B. (Dennys Watkins Pitchford) published by Mammoth/Reed. Reprinted by permission of David Higham Associates.

Extract from *Doctor Dolittle: A Treasury* © Hugh Lofting. First published in Great Britain by Jonathan Cape 1968. Reprinted by permission of Christopher Lofting c/o Ralph M. Vicinanza, Ltd.

Extract from *Moominpappa at Sea* © Tove Jansson, translated by Kingsley Hart. Reprinted by permission of A&C Black.

Extracts from *The True Confessions of Charlotte Doyle* by Avi, first published in the UK by Orchard Books, a division of the Watts Publishing Group, 96 Leonard Street, London EC2A 4RH. Reprinted by permission of the Publisher.

Extracts from *Kon Tiki and I* by Erik Hesselberg, first published by Allen and Unwin Ltd. Reprinted by permission of Harper Collins Publishers Ltd.

Extract from *We Didn't Mean to go to Sea* © the Estate of Arthur Ransome, published by Jonathan Cape. Reprinted by permission of Random House.

Extract from *Island of the Blue Dolphins* © Scott O'Dell 1960. (refer pages 52-59, 1966 Puffin ed.) Reprinted by permission of Penguin Books Ltd. 'Pirates on Funafuti' © The Estate of E. V. Rieu. Reprinted by permission of Dominic Rieu.

Extracts from *The Mermaid of Emmeloord* © Jan de Hartog 1966 from *The Call of the Sea* published by Hamish Hamilton. Reprinted by permission of Andrew Nurnberg Associates.

'An Uneventful Voyage' © Estate of Hilaire Belloc 1970. Reprinted by permission of The Peters Fraser and Dunlop Group Limited on behalf of The Estate of Hilaire Belloc

The Mystery of the Mary Celeste © Maurice Saxby 1998. Reprinted by permission of the author.

Every effort has been made to trace the copyright holders. The Publishers would like to hear from any copyright holder not acknowledged.

ILLUSTRATION CREDITS

Endpapers from *The Swiss Family Robinson* illustration © Mike Taylor, 1998

Bookplate (page 1) © Priscilla Lamont, 1998

Section One illustration detail (page 7) from 'A two-decker and a hoy becalmed off-shore' by Francis Sartorius. Courtesy of the Richard Green Galleries

The Wind in the Willows illustrations © Peter Rush, 1998

Boating illustration © L'uboslav Pal'o, 1998

The Little Grey Men illustrations © Mike Taylor, 1998

Moby Dick illustration detail from 'Portrait of the Royal Sovereign of 1701' by L. d. Man. Courtesy of F. B. Cockett Private Collection

The Voyages of Doctor Dolittle illustration © Priscilla Lamont, 1998

Moominpappa at Sea illustration © Liz Pyle, 1998

Section Two illustration detail (page 29) from 'A merchant barque picking up a pilot in Valparaiso Bay' by Thomas Jacques Somerscales

The True Confessions of Charlotte Doyle illustrations © Peter Rush, 1998

Kon-Tiki and I illustrations © Fiona Saunders, 1998

O to Sail illustration detail from 'An East Indiaman and shipping off Harwich' by John Thomas Serres. Courtesy of the Richard Green Galleries

The Jumblies illustrations © Gisèle Rime, 1998

We Didn't Mean to Go to Sea illustration © Priscilla Lamont, 1998

Section Three illustration detail (page 55) from 'The Loss of the Brig Warren near Teignmouth in Devon' by Thomas Luny

Robinson Crusoe illustrations © Peter Rush, 1998

The Rime of the Ancient Mariner illustration © Hannah Firmin, 1998

Twenty Thousand Leagues Under the Sea illustration © Jamel Akib, 1998

The Swiss Family Robinson illustration © Mike Taylor, 1998

Island of the Blue Dolphins illustration © Kathryn Prewett, 1998

What Pain it was to Drown illustration © Derek Pearson, 1998

Section Four illustration detail (page 81) from 'The Loss of the Brig Warren near Teignmouth in Devon' by Thomas Luny

The Adventures of Tom Sawyer illustrations © Peter Rush, 1998

The Coral Island illustrations © Kim Gamble, 1998

Pirates on Funafuti illustrations © Priscilla Lamont, 1998

Mary Read illustration detail from an untitled painting by Adrian van Diest. Courtesy of F. B. Cockett Private Collection

Treasure Island illustrations © Priscilla Lamont, 1998

Section Five illustration detail (page 107) from 'On the Lagune of Venice' by E. W. Cooke

The Mermaid of Emmeloord illustrations © Peter Rush, 1998

An Uneventful Voyage illustration © Dominique Falla, 1998

How the Whale Got His Throat illustrations © Zoe Kenway, 1998

The Mystery of the Mary Celeste illustration detail from 'A Stormy Day at Sea' by Bonaventura Peeters

Pages 123, 128 illustrations © L'uboslav Pal'o, 1998